Beneath The Willows

Hamlin County Series
Kate Blake

K Blake Publishing

Contents

Trigger Warnings

- *Previous domestic abuse/violence*

- *Flashbacks*

- *Death without specific details*

- *Grief*

- *PTSD*

- *Anxiety and Depression discussed*

- *Open-door explicit sexual scenes*

- *Detailed sexual encounters*

Author's Note

This story is entirely a work of fiction; the characters and all storylines were created by this author and her imagination. Any coincidental similarities to real-life events or people are just a coincidence.

Map of Maine

Created by Kate Blake

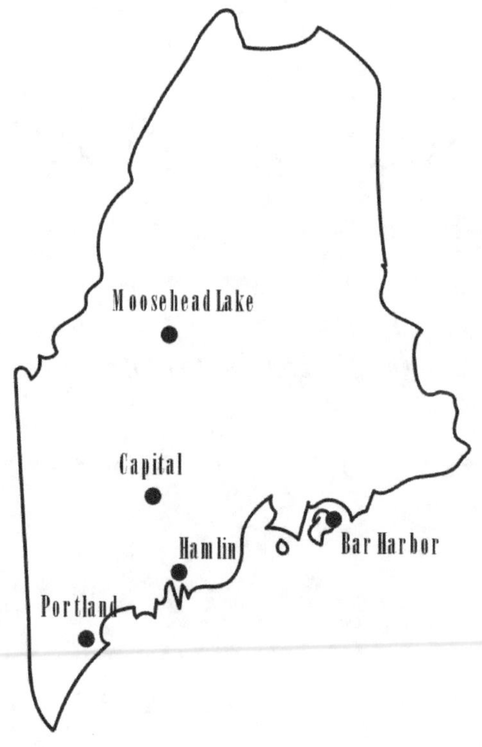

The map portrays the State of Maine with fictional towns and real towns. For the stories purposes I have created a map demonstrating where they are located.

Dedicated

To all the girls who thought that, they did not deserve a happily ever after, Do not give up on your own, happy ending.

Beneath The Willows

By: Kate Blake

Chapter One

Kira

Rolling the windows down in the car, the once familiar smell fills my nose. The scent I never missed until I was back here and would inevitably have to leave again. A flood of memories and mistakes fly through my mind as I make my way up Route One toward home. After ten years, I finally decided to come home. With Winston in my passenger seat, his head hanging out the window, he takes in the Atlantic Ocean, tasting and smelling. His tongue wags across his black-and-white mouth as we continue north. Winston has been with me on all my adventures; he is the perfect mix of a black lab and an Alaskan husky. His honey-brown eyes always knew how to ground me and make me feel at home.

About a month ago, my contract with the military ended, and I rode out my leave in the state I had called home for the last few years. Saying goodbye to a life that I lived for what felt like forever. I wasn't anyone special, not a Security Force member or a Crew chief, but I worked as an x-ray tech in the Air Force. I got all my licenses and retained all my certifications, planning to work as a tech when I came home… *But was I really ready for that? Could I face the town I left all those years ago? I did not leave on bad terms; with a shiver running down my neck, I recall the disappointment I experienced when I left—marrying the first man who made me feel pretty.*

I look into those honey eyes and let a big breath out. He somehow knows my exact pain. He was not here for the first year of that mess, but he was there for the end of it. Winston was always there to witness my life's darkest, saddest, and scariest moments.

There was another reason I was not incredibly excited to be home with all those friends who told me they would write, they'd visit. Well, they never did. In these ten years, I made it home to see my family whenever I could, and I even had visits from my mom, dad, and little brother every year, sometimes twice. So, twenty visits in ten years. I appreciated every visit, but it never felt like enough. Now, all of that would change; I would be home for good. I could rekindle old friendships and maybe even start new ones.

After just a few more hours of driving, I will be back in the little community of Hamlin. A beautiful coastal town. It has a New England vibe with shops along Main Street. The county is named after one of those old politicians from the 1800's. I am pretty sure he was Abraham Lincoln's vice president, but it really doesn't matter. A small town with friendly and welcoming people on the midcoast of Maine tucked away off the long Route One highway. If you were to hop southbound, you would end up in Florida. Another shiver…. Florida, yuck. No offense, Florida, but all your wildlife and I are not friends.

The sign comes into view, which I saw in the rearview mirror as my family and ex took me to the Military Entrance Processing Station (MEPS) in Portland. *The past is in the past.*

With just a few more miles to go, my phone rings. I touch the answer button on my steering wheel, "Kira, where are you? You were supposed to get here half an hour ago?" my mother says in her usual concerned voice.

"Almost there, Mom. I had to take a picture of the bridge when I got here and pee in Kittery." With a chuckle in the background, I know I am on speakerphone. My dad is making fun of me in the background for doing the "Instagram thing" and detailing my life experience with photos and small captions. "HI DADDY, SEE YOU SOON!" I yell into the space of my car.

"See you in a minute, Bunny," he says. The phone disconnects, and I turn down the winding road to the small ranch-style home where I grew up. Mom and Dad are waiting on the porch for me and Winston when we pull in. I open the door, and Winston goes barreling up the steps straight to my dad, the animal whisperer. They both hugged me and brought me into the living room. Then fussed over me for a few hours, getting me settled. My dad made my favorite home-blown popcorn, and we watched a Marvel movie until the exhaustion took over.

It only feels mildly embarrassing to be living with my parents again at the ripe age of 28. But here we are. A new start. Back where it all started. I lay in my childhood bed, which used to feel so huge but now feels incredibly small, with Winston spooning me and snoring. "Win, shhhh, roll over." I push him a little, but the trip was just as exhausting for him, too. Fourteen hours on the road with all the traffic, pee stops, and food. It felt like an eternity, but we made it. I'm slowly lulled into sleep and snuggle my noisy companion's neck.

I woke with a start. *Where the fuck am I,* "What the fuck" I said out loud. I am alone. The smell of booze and cigarette smoke filled my room. This cannot be real, "WINSTON!" I yell. No response, no clicks of nails on the linoleum floor; I looked down and realize where I am. A cold chill rolled over me; I am back here 9 years ago in the kitchen where I hoped I would never be again. All the adrenaline in my body floods through my veins; I need to get out of here. He cannot know that I am here or find me again. He would never let me go.

Anxiety engulfed me as my legs felt like lead. I need to get out of here.. I tried to make it to the discolored kitchen door; still peeling paint around the window. I reached for the doorknob and felt the warm, tight grip on my shoulder. He twisted me around, hard and fast...

Shooting straight up in my bed with a massive gust of breath, I try to get my bearings and figure out what just happened. I feel Winston's soft side against me, and I begin to breathe easier. It was a dream, a dream I stopped having five years ago with therapy, but it has returned just as I have.

***

Kira

At 4:30 in the morning, I slip out of my bed and reach for my phone. Padding out to the living room, Winston stalks behind me. I open the front door and sit on the glider while he goes for his morning pee. The sun is just about to rise; the air is cool and damp. Dew coats the grass and the vehicles in the front yard. Looking down at my phone, I have no new messages. No one checked in to ensure I made it home. Shocker, most of my friends in the service were not happy. I decided to leave for selfish reasons. Or I am being way too sensitive as usual. I laugh to myself, it is 5 a.m. I left yesterday, and I am sure I will hear from them today or tomorrow.

Walking back inside, I start the coffee pot and sit at the dining room table with my notebook, working on my checklist of everything I need to do now that I am home. I write "To Do" in a fancy script and start to doodle. Do I really want to be doing this early in the morning? So, I picked up my phone and scroll and scroll and scroll. Until I hear footsteps. My dad is up; he has always been an early riser. "Good morning, Bunny," he says with a sleepy smile on his lips.

"Morning, Daddy. Did you sleep well?" I get up and move into the kitchen with him. He gets his coffee and takes a big whiff; he does this every time, and I could watch him do it forever.

He looks up at me, "I slept great!" He takes a sip of coffee before turning back to me. "What would you like to do today? Do you want me to help you with stuff, or do you want to hang around the house?"

I look away. I don't know what I want to do. After that dream last night, my anxiety seems to have heightened. "I haven't decided yet, Dad. I was hoping to drive around the old back roads and get reacquainted with the town again, maybe go down to the Point and see the ocean crest off the road," I say quietly, with a small amount of hesitation in my voice.

Dad looks at me. He is a thinking man. It's usually something important, kind, or inquisitive when he speaks.

"Why don't we load up Winston and go do that? We'll go drive around and get lunch." "Then we can go down to the Point and sit on the rocks and watch." I nod; it is still super early, so I'm considering that plan.

"I'm going to lay back down for a while. Can he stay out here with you?" I say, pointing to Win.

"Yes, of course, I'll take him for a walk, and we can find the best poop spot in the yard."

I laugh because that's exactly what they are going to do. Padding off down the hall to my room, I get cozy under the oversized fluffy duvet that Mum bought me.

At around 9 a.m., Dad and I get into the four-runner I had to have before leaving Virginia. The vehicle is the deep olive green I have always wanted, with black trim everywhere. I had to have a black interior because it looked the best and because of Winston's fur.

First, we head down Route One to the old fishing hole in town. We go down to the old dock we used to jump off as kids. There is a boat launch made of concrete textured slabs and a float out in the water with a swirling blue slide. We chose to come here because of the smaller dock off to the side of the boat launch; that way, Win can jump off and chase sticks into the water. There are always some ducks, and he also loves to chase them. We exit the car, and Win is always bounding down the path headed straight for…. Yep, the ducks. "Be gentle!" I yell as if he can catch one. He may be almost a full-blooded retriever, but the husky in him doesn't help with his coordination. He is not one for catching living animals but sticks; that is where he shines.

After an hour of silence on the edge of the dock, my dad didn't say a word. He hasn't inquired why I decided not to take the massive sign-on bonus and stay in the military for another four years. I honestly didn't know why I didn't take it. *If I'm honest, I feel lost; how do you tell your parents when you are 28 years old that you have no idea who you are?* I criticize myself internally.

We head off to our next destination and load into the four-runner. "Where to next?" He asks with that familiar shine in his eyes. I decide to turn down the road and head for the downtown area. Downtown Hamlin is beautiful; there are buildings from the 1800s made with bricks laid by the hands of new Americans. There are shops with little hidden storage rooms from the old prohibition days and a bookstore. It is the bookstore I have loved my whole life, with white-washed brick with an old oak door. It smells like books and coffee, and with the cafe connected by an archway, I can buy my two favorite things in one place. But we aren't going to the bookstore today; we are headed to the Met, a sub shop that makes the best sandwiches, soups, and cookies around. I find that I may be biased, though, but only because they are my favorite, and I refuse to try any other shop's sandwiches.

"Maybe we can get something in town for lunch?" Turning my head to look at him, I already know where I want to eat and where I want to sit, "We can sit in the back parking lot on the benches and watch Win stare intently at the water."

My dad laughs, "That boy sure does love to look at fish, even in the kiddie pool out back." I laugh, too, because he isn't wrong.

Win is obsessed with staring into the water and thinking he will catch a fish with his teeth. Like he's some grizzly bear in the rivers of Alaska during the salmon mating season.

The sun is starting to rise in the sky, and the heat is warming my neck and hair. We decided to sit below one of the large pine trees. There are a few picnic tables set up along the shore; they are under the trees to provide a respite from the early summer sun. Winston is lounging below the table, and we sit and watch the waves crash over the large rock formations that make up the rocky coast of Maine.

My Dad, Jesse Russell Logan, was in the United States Air Force. He worked on AC130 gunship aircraft that fought in wars. They carried many men and women to and from safety. He left the service around his 9-year mark when he met my mom; their love story was beautiful and magical. After meeting through a friend, he whisked my British mother away from Europe and brought her home to America. I arrived on this earth as an accident that happened after far too much wine. They had been married for three years when they had me. I have always wanted to be loved the same way my Dad loves my Mom. Thinking that I will never find that scares me, and it hurts more than I care to admit; I take a breath, "Dad?"

He looks away from the crashing ocean. "Yes, sweetie?"

"I want to find a love like what you and Mom have, a love that came out of nowhere but was exactly what you both needed," I reply with tears tracing lines down my cheeks.

He looks at me as a small smile crosses his lips, "You will one day, sweetie; you just can't force it." *I know he is right, but after one failed marriage at 18, I have massive reservations about trusting anyone enough to let them love me or even think about loving them. My heart has been a vault since I was 21 years old. Sometimes, I think I have lost the combination.*

I look over at him, ready to confess how I feel: "I have just picked up my life and moved. I don't know what I want to do with my life, but what I do know is that I don't want to be alone anymore." I sigh. I want to let someone into my heart, to love me, and start a life with me. Though most people I grew up with already have their families and careers, I am starting from the beginning."

Tears continue to flow even harder now. He reaches over and pulls me into his arms. "You will figure it out, sweetie. There is no rush. Your mother and I love having you home. We will not have to drive anymore to come see you. I don't know if we would be able to make another 15-hour drive again." Why they would not just fly is beyond me, I think to myself.

"I know I will, but I guess what my question is, when will my life begin? I feel as though I have been in limbo for the last 8 years." I admit for the first time out loud to someone who isn't myself.

"Everyone's story starts on a different page, Kira." His eyes soften, seeing right through me.

He is me in the form of a man. I have his emotions, empathy, and understanding. I know he is right; I know that my story will begin one day. Maybe soon, *but I won't know unless I continue to turn the pages.*

I look back at him again and nod, "I know, Daddy; I'll get back on my feet and in a routine soon enough." We stood together and loaded Winston back into the car. On the drive back home, we pass the old mills with the bridge all the town kids jumped off in the summers and the downtown Main Street filled with people going about their business; we hop onto Route One again and make our way back to the little ranch I never thought I would be living in again.

Chapter Two

Ben

Pulling up to the job site down on Pem Point, I notice a few tourists are back in the area. They tend to flood this coastal paradise to look out at the crashing deep blue ocean and the centuries-old lighthouse that stands as a pillar of our excellent state's history along the coast of the Atlantic Ocean. The plumbers and electricians are hard at work opening all the cottages here. Most of the cottages along the Atlantic coast are seasonal; all the electricity is shut off, and the plumbing is drained to avoid freezing pipes; hundreds if not thousands of small and large cottages along Maine's coast are swamped. My crew and I are building a coastal cape for a seemingly nice couple from out of state. You never really know what you will get when you're not building with a local. With locals come the gossip mill. The gossip mill has not started up yet for the summer; it is only in the middle of May.

This job should be pretty cut and dry, a quick cape with a double dormered roof, something I have done a few times on this picturesque coastline. Today is my favorite; framing day. We are starting fresh on the new floor system, getting the walls up and square. My guys Chad and Muck are here; Chad is the muscle. He is good at lifting things and moving them. Listening and quickness are not his strongest qualities, but Muck is my site supervisor. He knows how to perform the tasks I need to complete and does it well. I look up to the deck of the floor system and shout, "All right, guys, let's lift these walls!" With that, we start our day.

I arrive home around 4 in the evening, and some sun is finally left in the sky after such a long, dark winter. I should have just enough sun left to reach even 8 p.m. before dark. I head out to the pad, which is a leveled-off area I use to perform maintenance and other projects on the equipment I own. I decided earlier in the day that I would get to work on my old John Deer tractor; regular maintenance is needed for the summer ahead, and working out here gives me the time I need to decompress from the day. Building is surprisingly stressful; coordinating material deliveries and being the main builder who knows exactly what they are doing takes it out of you.

Once the oil is changed and in good working order, I attach the forks to the bucket to move some material and do some much-needed spring cleaning. I live in an ancient single-story white house; it was built in the 60s, and it shows, which is fine because it's just me and my doofus of a chocolate lab, Crash. Crash fits her name; she came barreling into my life and has not slowed down since. She needed a home, and I needed some company.

Sometimes, I wonder what it would be like if I could find a woman. Someone I could see spending the rest of my life with. Unfortunately, I haven't found that yet because I live in an area with a larger tree population than actual people. This area is small; people talk and trying to find someone who has similar interests and the idea of a perfect life has been difficult. I have found that everyone has been with everyone in that way, and I am just not looking for that kind of drama. In high school, I kept my head down and did the classes I needed to get the job done so I could graduate and start my business. There are a few guys around here who started their own business at 17 and are still going strong doing what they love today, 11 years later.

I have noticed women, obviously, and had a few girlfriends here and there, but all those faded with the sun over the horizon. My brother has been in a relationship with the same girl for about 7 years, and they have broken up a few times. *I do not get it; if you found someone you love that you've spent this long time together, what is the wait? Why aren't they married?* It is almost like he's still be looking for the perfect girl; I don't think there is anyone more perfect for him. They are very similar and have similar professions; they agree on politics and enjoy each other's company. If I find a girl I know I could spend forever with, I would not make her wait forever to know that I am committed and want to marry her. *But…. Will I find her?*

Once the chores are complete and the yard is cleared of sticks with the help of Crash, we make our way back inside for a much-needed lie-down in bed for the night, which is just my crazy girl and me. "You're all I need, Crash," she lifts her head and sighs loudly. Flopping back down in response, I feel the love.

***

Kira

I have been home for a whole week; I have applied to the local hospital in town and found a possibility for a short-term apartment rental until I can get the perfect house. Also, I have avoided going to the grocery store like the plague. As it was my first job in high school and it's where all the busybodies get their gossip, I refuse. Handing my mother the grocery list, she asks if I want to join her. I hand her my credit card as well and shake my head. "You know people already know you're home; you post everything on Instagram." She tells me with a look of confusion; *I know this; of course, I do. Do I want to see anyone I grew up with, or is the possibility of seeing anyone I know just not it?*

I shiver, "No, Mom, I'm good; until I am living alone again, I'll let you get them for me." I grin sheepishly, "Maybe even then, I'll have you do it for me." My mother rolls her eyes and heads out the front door. Nora Marie Logan, a charge nurse at the hospital, the very one I applied to, is also the best mom a girl could ask for. Her and Dad's relationship is solid, and they gave my brother and I a safe and fulfilling childhood. We never wanted anything and always had what we needed. We were not spoiled, but we weren't poor either. My Dad, who also works in medicine, gave me that medicine bug.

It all started when I was twelve years old; I almost broke my arm and had to have an X-ray. I screamed at the woman who tried straightening my arm on the table. I thought it was broken, and she was about to break it even more. I was wrong, not even a crack. After that, I had the X-ray bug; it was not that I wanted to cause people pain, but having the ability to see exactly what was going on inside someone's body was incredible. I fell in love with the field immediately. I fell even harder once I started in the Air Force and learned all the physiology and pathology that could happen to a person's bones. My relationship with my ex-husband was a mess, but the constant in my life was my patients. My work kept that broken part of me together, knowing I was doing everything possible to help someone suffering and in pain.

When I was in Ohio at WPAFB, there were times when work was not the sanctuary I hoped it would be. When you are competing to make rank with other people who are just as qualified, and you must pass test after test, things get stressful. My relationship was a dumpster fire, and work was getting more stressful, so I acted out. I had an attitude with higher-ups and did not take people's criticism well... So when I got orders to leave, I took it. I ended up in Virginia at LAFB.

Hampton Roads, VA, was where I met Evelyn. She was also an X-ray tech, but she was a civilian. I was not competing with her; I wasn't trying to make rank alongside her. She was just my Eve, my confidant and best friend when everything in my life went wrong. Before I got orders to Virginia, I filed for divorce. I was free and single with the best friend I could have ever asked for. When I left VA, a part of us was ripped and broken, as if our friendship couldn't last the distance between us. There were so many miles, so little time in a day. I hope that one day we can repair that friendship we once had, but being so far away... I do not know if we can do it.

When I wasn't working on base or with Eve, I was with Winston; it was always just him and me. He didn't care about what we went through; he only saw me as his person. I am who loves him, feeds him, and takes care of him. He didn't care that I loved to paint or loved to read; he didn't ask all the stupid dating questions to get to know me. He loves me, sitting here now watching him sleep I realize that coming home was a good decision, but I need to open myself up to new experiences and things.

I look up at the sound of the doorbell, and the door swings open. Oliver strides in, lanky and tall, just as I remember the last time I saw him. "KIRA!" He shouts as I jump from the couch for a big bear hug. He is taller than me, but I probably weigh more than him. He is a brilliant, sensitive, and loyal baby brother. Ollie has always been there, but I could not tell him everything because, like me, he is quick to anger. So I kept a lot of it to myself.

"Ollie! I am so glad you are here. Do you want to get lunch?" I hope we can leave this town and go to the capital or down south.

"I was thinking we go to Portland. Get some seafood and coleslaw." He looks at me with a straight face.

I gag, "Do not even start."

"What?" he says, his voice full of sarcasm. "Are you still not over that incident?"

"You know exactly why I will not be eating seafood!" I looked with a huff.

"One bad experience isn't a reason to avoid the entire food group." He chastises me.

"You didn't see the lobster's little face and eyes when he was dropped into the pot." I can still hear their tiny screams and the steam taking their life. "Nope, I'm good."

"Fine, Olive Garden in the capital?" He says with more enthusiasm.

"YES!" Oh, the calories; everyone needs carbs to make life better. I could drown in the Alfredo sauce alone. Mmmmm, and those breadsticks. Ollie clears his voice; I look up, forgetting I am not alone with my thoughts. "Sorry, well, not really. I love me some alfredo sauce."

"Me too. Now let's get out of here," he says over his shoulder as he makes his way out the door.

***

Ben

As the summer weather returns, so do the out-of-staters. They are now in full swing. That means more people in our quiet little town. The days are getting longer and warmer every day, I am not excited about the heat, but it is much better than freezing my butt off while hanging siding on the house with cedar clapboards in below-freezing real-feel temperatures. The guys have been working hard; there has been a lot of progress. The customers seem happy, and the framing process is fast, but the steps between here and drywall are slow.

I could use a distraction or a date. I have been on those dating apps before and have not had much luck. *The women I have dealt with recently don't care that I built my own business at 17 years old; they don't care that I am not a drinker and I don't smoke. The women I have spoken to also don't care that I am the nice guy. I want nothing more than to give someone love and to be loved in return. These women... My goodness*

I thought I knew everyone in our small community. Apparently, I was mistaken. There are some seriously weird women around here. One woman wanted me to tie her up and pretend I was there to hurt her... A shiver rolls over me as I remember the absolute shock, then the immediate deletion of the app.

It has been quite a few months since I was on Tinder; that last experience I had was not something I wanted to repeat. I'm going to give this new app a try. It has been making waves on social media and even on the news because of its ability to find your match. It limits men's ability to talk to any woman they match to because the ladies hold all the power. They must message us before we can message them. So, later that evening, I do just that: post an older picture of Crash and me and write a little about me. Ladies love the dog dad pictures. I'm not sure if I want something serious or some fun. Guess we'll see how it turns out. Swiping right, we like them, and swiping left, we do not, easy enough. I think, *nope, nope, nope, nope, what am I even looking for here?* With a sigh, I go to close my phone and wait a minute.

Kira, I know a girl named Kira. I went to high school with her. *Looking back, she was just as adorable then as she is now. She was with the wrong crowd, though, the loud annoying "hick" guys. How is it that quiet, respectful guys never get the girl? I remember having one conversation with her, one word on both sides. I saw her in the hallway during class; I was headed to my locker, and who knows where she was going. She looked at me and smiled, "Hey" was all she said to me, and that was that.* All I know about her now is that she left town right after high school, and I haven't seen her in a decade. Now, I am intrigued.

Chapter Three

Kira

Oh man, I've started work and decided against the apartment. There wasn't any real reason to run away from my parents when I just got home. Except I think I need a social life. I might be messing with my parents, *gag* mojo, or groove. I need to be out of the house more. Meet new people, or maybe I don't know, get laid? So here I am, sitting on the back porch, Winston and my dear friend, a cold glass of Riesling to make great decisions tonight. I laugh out loud because this was our routine when we also lived in Virginia. So, I decide, with my glass of wine in hand, to take the dating app plunge. I have been back and forth the last few days, and the girls at work are wonderful. They tell me to "DO IT, GIRL!"

"Get out there!" I am their entertainment since they are all married or in serious relationships.

It is 8 o'clock, and the sun is still out; people wonder why I miss winter; when it gets dark early, I don't need an excuse to go lay in my bed and pass out at 7:30 p.m. Here I am, there is still sun out in the sky, and I may or may not be making a huge mistake. I tried every app possible after my divorce. I tried and tried to figure out what was wrong with me, that Avery would have cheated. Not just with someone where we were in Ohio but in Maine, too. *Who has the fucking time?* After several dates, that usually led to more because I needed to know if it was me. Did I do it wrong? Were there things I could improve on?

After years of therapy in a chair and on my back, I roll my eyes to myself. I found out it wasn't me, nope! I just married a psychopath/narcissist; apparently, according to my therapist, it's far too common to be distracted by a charming, charismatic personality. To then be swindled into thinking, holy shit, this man loves me. Nope, Kira, wrong again.

So, one more sip of this delicious wine, and boom. I launched my profile with some cute pictures of me and some with Winston, so these guys know that I do not just care for myself, but I have kept my handsome furball alive for 10 years! *Also, who does not love a cute blonde with a pup? Everyone, that's who! Keep your confidence up, Kira; you've got this. I worked through a lot of my self-confidence issues with my therapist and my trust issues, which I still need to work on.* So, I need to swipe right if you like them and swipe to the left if I don't; *that's pretty standard. Here we go; nope, nooo, absolutely not. I used to change his diapers! He is not twenty-five or older... Nope, nope, nope. Wait, what is this? I know that name, Benjamin. I worked at the grocery store with his brother.* Oh, he has a dog too! They could play! All right, let's do this. This is the app that we, the ladies, get to message first. I swipe right and cross my fingers; how crazy would it be if he. A message "YOU'VE MATCHED" pops up on the screen, and I stifle a squeal! He likes me! Or, well, he liked my profile enough to swipe right. I will send him a quick "Hey stranger" message, not to forward but not too casual. *Do not overthink this, Kira, as I cross my fingers.* It is now 10 p.m., and he's probably not even awake.

***

Ben

PING, I open one eye and look at my phone. "YOU'VE MATCHED!" I open both eyes now; *who did I match with? Kira Logan messaged me, too.* Looking into the chat, I see she said, "Hey, Stranger," *I look at the time it's 10 p.m. I am not starting a conversation this late. I have trusses coming in the morning; I need as much sleep as possible to ensure Chad and Muck do not fall off the building. I closed my phone and rolled over. I will message her in the morning, maybe?...*

***

Kira

I am lying in bed. It was around 11:30 p.m., and Benjamin didn't message me back. These hopes and disappointments are why I hate using these apps. The messages don't show if they read my message or not. I will go to sleep and wait for the morning to come and not get my hopes up.

We never talked in high school. I remember that Benjamin Barnett was quiet and reserved and worked hard to become a builder. I was too distracted by the boys around me in my friend's circle and the fact that I was leaving. I rest my head gently on my pillow and close my eyes, thinking that maybe I shouldn't have been so focused on those guys around me. Who knows, maybe I would've saved my heart 2 years of pain and suffering.

I wake startled, but I am not really awake. I'm here again, on the cold linoleum floor. The smell of cigarettes and whiskey tinged the air, and I was alone. Winston is not here. I slowly try to stand my legs again, feeling like lead; I make my way over to the door. My hand is almost to the knob when that warm terrifying grip grabs my shoulder and spins me around. Those terrifying eyes with the pupils completely dilated, I cannot even see the once gentle forest green eyes. Once gentle, Kira, he was never gentle. You were just blind, I chastise myself. I can smell his breath; he is drunk, and it is pouring out of his skin as he breathes inches from my face. "Where the fuck do you think you're going" he spits out.

"I, we, I'm leaving." *This is a dream; it must be a dream. This is not real; you're free. WAKE UP, KIRA...*

"The fuck you are, we're going to work this out," He cheated again. There was nothing to fix, "It happened once, baby girl; I won't do it again." His voice is gentle, but I know it is just an act. I never went against him when this happened; I just let it happen. *Not today, not again.!*

"FUCK YOU," I spit out, turn in his grip, and run. *Well fuck*, I try to run. *GASP!* I suck in the biggest breath, waking up from that nightmare drenched in sweat again. What the hell is happening? *Why are the dreams coming back again?* I wonder as I check the time; again, it is 4:30 in the morning, and I'm awake.

Awake before the sun, Winston and I make our way outside. We both needed the air, and he had to take care of his business. I check my usual social media and take a picture of dew on the long blades of uncut grass. Posting it with the caption "up before the sun, before the dew has had time to dry." I checked the dating app but had no luck. He has not messaged, so maybe he's sleeping. Or maybe he's as nervous as me about starting a conversation with a practical stranger. I stifle a sigh of disappointment I am feeling.

***

Ben

It is 5 a.m. I have made my coffee, checked my emails, organized my material slips, and watched an entire episode of my favorite YouTube guy. There is not much to do now but sit and wait for the sun to emerge from the horizon and shove off to work. I pulled out my phone and opened the dating app. *Is it too early to message her? Will she think it is weird I am up so early? Also, why do I care if she thinks I am weird for being an early riser? I don't even know her yet.* I chastise myself for overthinking. I decided I would wait; I would message her at a reasonable hour when most people are awake. I do not even know what she does for work or her routine yet, so I think it's a safe bet to wait. 8 a.m. it is; I do not want to get sucked into a long conversation, so I'll chat with her and see where it takes us. I resigned myself from that decision and turned YouTube back on.

***

Kira

PING! I look up from the book I've been reading while waiting for patients to come into the department for an X-ray. It is 8:15 a.m., and there is a message waiting for me from Ben. Ekk, I squeal to myself while doing the happy dance in my chair. "Hey to you to stranger" comes up in the chat. Play it cool, Kira. You *got this*.

> Kira 08:17 [Long time no see. How have you been?]

How long will it take for a response? He is a well-known builder in our area and is probably busy. "PING!" My eyes go wide, and there it is: "Yes!" I whisper-yell aloud because he messages immediately.

> Ben 08:20 [It has been a while; I've been great. Work has been busy.]

Ben 08:21 [Are you back for good? What has it been? 10 years.]

Kira 08:22 [That's great! I am back for good. Deciding if it was the right choice. Adulting is hard.]

Why am I so boring? Do not overthink this; speak. Be confident, for God's sake!

Kira 08:25 [I wanted to know what you thought about us chatting via texts instead of this app since we are already friends on social media?]

Ben 08:26 [I was going to ask you the same thing!]

Ben 08:26 [My number is 207-555-0820]

Kira 08:26 [Perfect, see you there!]

"See you there" *What the fuck, why would I say that?* Sighing to myself, I click out of the dating app and over to my messenger app. I'll shoot him a quick text now.

Kira 08:27 [Long time no talk!]

Facepalm, *why am I like this? Maybe he'll like it; I think I'm charming.* Haha. I laugh to myself in the most self-deprecating laugh I can muster. "CHIMES," the sound of my messenger app grabs my attention. Looking down, it is him.

> Ben 08:30 [So, Kira tell me about yourself. What do I need to know to truly get to know you?]

Shock, I am well and in shock right now. He started an actual conversation with me. Please don't ask me stupid questions like, "Tell me your favorite color or how many men you've slept with." No, he wants to know who I am. He wants me to tell him about myself *and what I can do.* I chastise myself. *I can talk about myself, right? Do I give him all of it or just some bits and pieces?*

> Kira 08:35 [Well, I was in the Air Force for the last ten years. I have been married once before and divorced. I have a black lab named Winston; he is ten years old. He is my ride-or-die, and we both live at my parents' house. The one I grew up in.]

Kira 08:36 [I love reading, painting, singing, and relaxing. I am an eternal homebody and plan to stay that way forever.]

Kira 08:37 [What about you, Benjamin? What do you need me to know about you? What is your story?]

Ben 08:39 [I'd love to give you the long version after work if that is okay. I'll give you the short version now. I'm a home builder; I have a chocolate lab, Crash. She is six years old. Lastly, I own my own home.]

Ben 08:40 [I get off at 4:00 p.m. :D]

Kira 08:40 [Okay! I'll talk to you then!]

***

Ben

Looking down at my phone, I see that it is finally 4 p.m., and I'm unsure if I should text her now or wait a little bit longer.

Fuck it, I have been thinking about her all day. I even found myself scrolling her Instagram on my lunch break. *She takes a lot of pictures, but they are not all just of herself.* I think to myself while I continue to scroll. There is everything here: her food, her dog, and the places she has traveled. There are a few selfies, and I find myself looking into her ocean-blue eyes, which are dark and inviting. She has honey blonde, shoulder-length hair and a different pair of glasses in every single picture. Are they real glasses or prescription? I will have to ask her myself.

After about five minutes of wavering, I decided to text her. I want to know everything there is to know about her, which is incredibly odd. Usually, I am not the invested type. She is something new, though, beautiful, and wants to talk to me.

Ben 16:06 [Hey, Kira! Hope you had a great day!]

Kira 16:06 [Hey Ben! I did, and you made it even better now.]

Ben 16:07 [Is that so? What did you do today? What exactly do you do for work?]

Kira 16:08 [Oh, I am an X-ray Technologist. I look at broken bones and x-ray them. I only worked a half day today. I found a broken finger and ankle. For the rest of the day, though, I have been lounging on the back porch with a book and Winston.]

Ben 16:10 [An X-ray Tech? That is awesome; I could use you on the job sites. Is Winston a high-energy pup?]

Kira 16:15 [Oh yes! Bring them on in when they're hurt. Win is the best dog ever! He is therapy dog trained and licensed as a service dog for me.]

Ben 16:16 [That is great! Crash is wild most of the time. Do you mind me asking why he's a service dog?]

Kira 16:18 [Of course, I have panic attacks and anxiety. He can sense when I am feeling anxious and comes to put his head down on my lap. I don't bring him everywhere I go; I don't want him to work 24/7.]

Ben 16:21 [What a handsome boy! Here is Crash]

Kira 16:22 [Oh! She is super cute too! Also, I have a question...?]

Ben 16:22 [Yes...?]

Kira 16:23 [How do you feel about Facetime? Or are you just a phone call kind of guy?]

Ben 16:25 [Umm... Well, I'm going to say no to Facetime. Only because I've never done it before, and it would probably be awkward and weird. Let me get a few things done and eat. Then I'll give you a call around 7?]

Well, that was a short but good talk! We both love our jobs and have dogs. I do not know how to behave on Facetime, though. Do I look at myself? Or do I look at her? Will she think I am attractive or just quiet and awkward? But, if we could FaceTime, I would be able to see her and her reactions to what I have to say. I can learn about her mannerisms and responses. I will get to see her. Hmmmm. "Alright, Crash, chores, then dinner!" Her head snaps up, and she is off. Running at top speed toward the house, I yell to her, "SLOW DOWN!" As I say it, she looks over her shoulder at me and trips over some sticks. THUD! She gets up quickly like nothing happened and bolts into the house through the

doggy door.

nothing happened and bolts into the house through the

doggy door.

48

Chapter Four

Kira

That went well, I think, after I put my phone down from talking to Ben. *Right?* I am home alone for a bit longer. I throw some laundry in for my parents and start dinner. Opening the fridge, I realize there is not much to choose from. There is chicken and some heavy cream; I decide that I'll make chicken paprika like my dad used to when I was a kid. It is one of the many meals I taught myself to make to make me less homesick.

I dice an onion and chop the chicken into smaller pieces to help it cook quicker. After the onions began to turn translucent, I add the paprika and chicken. I continue with the recipe until I hear the front door open and shut.

"Kira, we're home! It smells wonderful." My dad yells from the front door. The two of them work at the hospital together and work the same days so they can spend time together on their days off. They drive to and from work together and are so freaking cute sometimes. The three of us gather around the dining table as I grab dinner.

"How was your day, Kira? Are you enjoying the new hospital and change of pace?" Mom asks; she knows how rough it was for me in Virginia. We were so busy all the time. There were motor vehicle accidents and gunshot wounds daily, which did not help with the amount of anxiety I had already. Hamlin Memorial is a quiet, small county hospital. I have never seen or heard of a gunshot wound that wasn't hunting-related in my entire life. Motor vehicle accidents (MVA), on the other hand, are far more frequent, with drunk drivers and deer finding their way onto a 65-mph road. We are also a take-off point for LifeFlight. When there are significant scary accidents, they get diverted, or they get airlifted upon arrival here.

"Great! I only worked a half to cover a coworker's appointment." I say with a little too much excitement in my voice. My mother raises an eyebrow.

"Oh, really? Are you that excited about working for five hours?" There it is. She can smell gossip a mile away.

"Yes, Mum, I did have a great day," I say with less excitement in my tone. "I enjoyed reading my book most of the day, and during the rest of it, I relaxed with Winston."

"Leave it, Nora. She's happy; let her be happy." My dad says this, knowing exactly what my mom is getting at. We will see if she drops it; that would be a first for my mom.

"Fine, fine. She will tell me sooner or later. Something will go wrong, and she will need my advice." My mother shrugs. We finish dinner in a comfortable silence; I take a quick shower and turn the laundry over. It is almost 7 p.m., and I am buzzing. *Why am I so excited to talk to him? I never said a word to him in high school.*

After extensive social media stalking, I produced his business and Facebook pages with little to no activity. His profile picture is of himself and Crash. He has dark brown hair and is about 6 feet tall, maybe? I cannot see his eyes, but maybe one day, I'll get close enough to them to see them. Crash is a chocolate lab. I'm pretty sure a pure breed. He was quiet all those years ago; I wonder if he still is. I need normal, peaceful, calm, and loving. I do not have a lot of boxes to check off in a partner, but I do have a few.

I settle into my full-sized bed, with Winston already dozing off beside me. He's surprisingly quiet tonight. There is no obnoxious snoring to contend with. As I tuck myself in and rest my head on the pillow, my phone begins to ring in my hand. The name Ben Barnett pops up on the screen, and the default ringtone of soothing sounds plays out loud. I clear my throat and pick up the call.

"Hello," I say with a chipper voice.

"Hey Kira, how's it going," Ben's smooth masculine voice vibrates through the phone.

"Great, decided to get cozy for the phone call. Also, Winston got in bed before me, looking so sweet. I had to join in on the snugs." I grimace. Was that too much information? I hear a low laugh in the background,

"Well, I am just lying on the couch. Crash is sprawled out on top of me. It is one of her favorite places to nap." He tells me, and I bark out a laugh.

"I can only imagine that girl is squishing you?" *I am amazed that he allows her to do that*. The phone goes quiet for a second. "Ben?" I ask tentatively.

"Oh, I am right here; check your phone. I sent you the evidence of our cuddle session." There is that warm laughter again. I pull the phone away from my ear and devour the picture before me. It is indeed Ben, *my God. He is handsome; he has a beard now! Boy, do I have a soft spot for beards?* I haven't dated a man with a beard before, or my ex-husband was a child and couldn't grow anything on his face, and the rest of the men who have warmed my bed have all been military guys. Either they have the ugliest porno stash, or they are clean-shaven; there was not an in-between. "Would you look at that? She is crushing you. Can you breathe?" I say with a hint of sarcasm in my voice.

"Of course, I can breathe. She is not that heavy and so stinking cute when asleep. It is the only time I can stand her." He laughs low and deep, "I love the girl, but my god, she can be a handful or two." Now I am laughing because he is funny and sweet in the most unexpected way. I have spoken to a guy who is okay with sending selfies of him and his dog. He does not seem like a selfie-taking man.

I get up the courage to finally ask what I want. "So, Ben, what exactly are you looking for here?" I held my breath because maybe that was too far.

"Well, Kira, I am looking for friendship and companionship. I want to spend time with someone who likes to spend time with me. Someone who enjoys my company even if it is silent. I am not a huge talker, but when it's someone I'm comfortable with, I have no issue opening up. I want to be in a relationship one day, but I would be lying if I said I was not interested in a physical relationship." He says it like he means every single word. *My brain is in a frenzy; he wants companionship, but he also wants to spend time with someone who can just be quiet together. My God, is this a dream?* "What is your idea of fun? Do you go out and party?" I ask a little too sharply.

"No, Kira, I don't party, I don't drink, smoke, or do drugs." His voice was a little stern; maybe I was too sharp. He takes another breath, "I'm easy. I like to work on my equipment, lay in my hammock, and relax. I have a physically taxing career, so I am not about to stay up partying till God knows when. I am in bed by 9:30 p.m." He says it with such finality to his voice.

Did I make him mad? Did I ruin this already? I do not speak for a minute, "I'm sorry, Ben, I didn't." He cuts me off.

"Why on earth are you apologizing?" He asks, sounding surprised.

"Well, I made a pig-headed assumption that obviously offended you, and I'm a serial apologizer," I say quietly.

"Kira, you don't ever have to apologize for asking a question, especially with me." He explains, "It's my fault that I reacted before I had a minute to hear what exactly you were asking." He goes quiet for a few moments. "I should be the one to say sorry. I don't party, and I am a pretty relaxed guy."

Well then, I like him already, "I don't party at all; I barely drink." I say, "I have had the same bottle of wine in the fridge for the last two weeks; I have to get the kind my parents don't like so they won't drink it. Which means I don't really want to drink it either." With a chuckle in my voice this time. "My only real hobbies are reading, spending time with Winston, and napping. I am a sucker for a long cozy nap." He seems to mull over my response.

"Kira, you and I will get along just fine; now we have to find out if Crash and Winston have the same opinion of each other as we do." I laughed aloud this time because he is funny. *I could see us laughing together for a really long time.*

Please slow down, Kira; you have spoken to him for 10 minutes of your life. You aren't getting married.

"Winston is not really a new doggy person, like how some people are not people persons. He does not like other dogs for more than a few hours." I wonder if he can hear the smile in my voice, "He might have picked up some of my bad habits when it comes to being anti-social." *It is true; I only really have the energy for one person at a time, and it usually isn't for long periods during the day. I know myself, and he knows himself. We are each other, people/dogs; that is just how it's been for the last ten years.*

After about 25 minutes of getting to know each other, Ben and I decide to get ready for bed, and he promised to text me in the morning.

"Good night, Kira. Sweet dreams," He says in his sexy, masculine voice. *Mmmm.*

"You too, Ben," I say, almost breathless, eww. *I am just tired; that's all.* "Bye," I say and hang up the phone before he can say bye back. *I'm not sure why I do this, but I do it often, not just to random men I just started talking to.* "CHIMES," the messenger notification goes off almost immediately after I hung up.

Ben 21:25 [Um, rude. I didn't even get to say goodbye.]

Kira 21:25 [OH! I'm sorry, but it is a bad habit I have. I have been doing it for as long as I can remember. I don't do well with goodbyes, and I'm unsure why. Sorry again!]

Ben 21:26 [It's okay; there's no need to apologize. I just wanted to make sure you were okay and weren't upset. I'll text you in the morning. Do you have a preferred hour?]

Kira 21:26 [Well, I am not functioning before 7 a.m. I might be awake enough to talk to once I have had my coffee ha-ha.]

Ben 21:28 [You got it! I'll text around 7:30 p.m. to really let that caffeine sink in!]

Kira 21:30 [Perfect! Goodnight Ben, talk to you soon!]

Ben 21:30 [Good night, Kira!]

***

Kira

I feel the old linoleum again and the smells. Why subconscious! Are we really doing this again? I stand on my leaden legs and approach the peeling, discolored front door again. I do not have to be surprised for a third time; his tight grip twists me around. I spit out, *"WHAT!"* before he can get a word in edge-wise. *"WHY ARE YOU HERE?"* I am screaming; I do not care anymore. I am not scared, and I am not doing this again. The shrillness of my voice must affect him somehow because he releases me and steps back. His eyes are dilated, and the grimace is almost palpable. I feel the anger rolling off him.

"You are not going anywhere, Kira; you don't get to make decisions. You are mine," He growls menacingly. Taking a cautious step forward, he reaches for me. I do the only thing I can. I rear back a sock him square in the jaw. His eyes are surprised as he tips backward, almost in slow motion. With him distracted by pain, I turn on my heel and rip the

disgusting door open. I am barefoot, and it is cold; frost coats the grass. I turn around, and the doorway to the old apartment is empty, with the door hanging open. It is eerily quiet; he did not chase me out here. I am going to do that stupid thing people do in the movies. I slowly make my way back to the door. Peering into the doorway, I see that there is no one in the kitchen. I tip-toe slowly into the dining room; the old, dirty, tan carpet gives much-needed relief to my frozen toes. Stepping slowly, I look around; there is no sign of him. *Sniffle* I hear coming from the ajar door leading to what once was the only bedroom in this tiny apartment. I make my way over and slowly push it open; I can still hear... What is that? Crying, I look in, and there he is, sitting on the edge of the bed. His head is hanging down in his hands, chest racking with sobs.

"*Avery,*" I say so quietly and hesitantly that I do not even think the words can be heard. No, he heard me and turned his head towards me. His eyes were surrounded by red, and his face was wet with tears. I have never lived or seen this dream in my life. Usually, there is a scary scene that I never want to witness again.

"I don't know why I did it; I don't know how I did that to you." He cries quietly; I have never once received an apology.

"Oh, well, I don't know why you did it either," I say with more confidence in my voice.

*"Kira, I did those awful things to you, I hurt you, I ruined what we could have been." *Sniffle* God, he is crying again. What the fuck is this. I genuinely do not know how to react. I… I am so sorry I did this."*

"Um, thank you." I am utterly shocked that I am hearing these words.

"I cannot change what I did, but I… I am sorry." He says with finality.

Sucking in huge breaths, I sit up in my childhood bedroom again, I am not sweating, and Winston does not even stir. I have no fucking idea what just happened, but I think, did Avery Lark just apologize to me. I don't even know what to think; I don't even want to think about what happened in our past. I look at my phone. It is only 1 a.m. this time. I can go back to sleep; it was not only a terrifying nightmare but also a resolution to all my doubts. My inability to get past that might have been the problem.

I doubt that if Avery Lark is still in the area, but if he is, he definitely wouldn't be apologizing or attempting to make amends with anyone. He came back to Maine the day after I asked him for a divorce, and I haven't seen him in 8 years. He returned and spread lies about me, and then got a job in Alaska, supposedly on a king crab boat in the Baring Sea. No one from around here has seen him since. He doesn't have any family left in the state; they've all either moved away or passed away while I was gone. That's what the Hamlin Times said, the only newspaper I kept reading while I was gone. I needed some information about my hometown.

I rolled over, almost contented with the fact that I was okay, I was safe, and I was not the issue. I hoped to fall into a dream of fantasy and romance since I needed that in my life right now, even if it was fictional. I reached my arm around Winston; he did not so much as stir as I snuggled in for the next four hours when my alarm went off. We will start Thursday off right, not waking up early and drenched in sweat.

Chapter Five

Ben

I wake up at my regular 4:30 a.m. alarm to get to work on paperwork and drink my coffee. I have been unable to push Kira Logan out of my head; she was there when I closed my eyes, and my first thought was when I woke up. I know I shouldn't text her this early and that we talked about waiting till 7:30, but this is the first time I am this eager to speak to a woman. Her voice is sweet, not too high pitched, but not low in a masculine way. Her laugh is incredibly contagious, making me want to kiss her even more. *I could just Facetime her. I want to see her smile; perhaps that will put one on her face.*

I waited till 7:30 a.m., but I decided to call her instead of text her; that way, I could explain that I was at work already and just wanted to say good morning. Yes, that is what I'll do. I open my phone and click on her name, taking in her beautiful face in the contact photo; it's right in my recent calls. The only number in my phone that is not work-related or my mother's. It begins to ring and ring; maybe she isn't a morning phone call person.

"Ben! Hi, sorry I was in the shower." She yells a little; the shower squeaks off in the background. Bringing a smile to my face, she is probably naked. Heat fills my entire body and runs down to my groin.

"Do not be sorry! I just assumed I would call and say good morning instead of texting. I enjoyed our conversation last night and thought it might be nice." I express to her, sounding a little sheepish.

"Oh, it's no trouble; I am glad you called! How did you sleep?" she adds.

"Like the dead," I laugh under my breath. "How about you?" I ask.

"I had the most bizarre dream that usually turns into a nightmare, but it didn't this time." She says, sounding a little confused. "Otherwise, I slept till my alarm today, and I'm headed to work at 8 a.m."

"That's weird. Do you usually have weird dreams?" I ask hesitantly.

"You know, I haven't had one in a long time—like five years without this brand of nightmare." She tries to explain, still sounding confused, almost as if she is lost in her thoughts.

"Well, I am still glad you could sleep through the night otherwise. I have to get the guys going on the next stage of this building this morning. Can I call you later?" I insist.

"Yes, please! I get off work at 4:30, so any time after that works for me. Have a wonderful day!" I can hear her smile in her voice, and it warms my chest. The thoughts of her naked in the bathroom drifted away as I pictured her eyes scrunching on the sides with her mouth smiling wide.

"Have a great day too!" I say, meaning every word.

***

Kira

That was the best surprise I've had in a while. I heard my phone chiming while my hair, face, and eyes were covered in shampoo under the shower head. No one ever calls me, so I thought it was an emergency. I rinsed as fast as I did in basic training and leaped out of the shower. Drying my hands, I looked at my phone, and it was none other than Benjamin Barnett. I am still buzzing after the quick phone call; I got lost in my brain for a minute, thinking about what happened in my dreams last night. Those thoughts faded as the conversation continued, and he promised to call me later today.

I pad into my room, still pretty damp; my towel-off job did not work well. I laugh self-deprecatingly; I do not know why I didn't just take more care drying off, but I am not going back into that bathroom. I change into my black scrubs and slide into my favorite lavender New Balance sneakers. Grabbing my keys, phone, badge, and wallet, I head out to work. Mom and Dad are already there and will be back home before me today. I hop into my four-runner and drive to the hospital, daydreaming about kissing the crap out of Ben.

It is a hazy, warm Thursday evening as I make my way out through Hamlin. It is 4:30., and I am just waiting for the call, wondering if he really meant it or maybe he forgot about me. I do get like this; I'm up and end up disappointed in the end. Instead of stewing on the fact that it is only one minute past the time he told me he'd call, I listen to Taylor Swift's *"Wildest Dreams."* As I bellow out the chorus, I get out the last word, and my car switches to a call chime. I was so excited that I smashed the answer button before it rang.

"Hello!" I say with far too much enthusiasm.

"Oh, Kira, um, it didn't even ring." He sounds a little concerned.

"Yeah, it interrupted my terrible car singing, so I figured, why wait." I do not care that I am eager; I have been waiting all day to talk to him.

"That is totally fine. I wanted to ask you what you have going on this weekend. Are you busy on Saturday?" He asks without hesitation this time.

"I am hanging out with you!" I quip. It's fine, Kira; *he wants to hang out with you. I am reasoning with myself while I wait for his response.*

"Is that so? What are we doing then, Kira? Do you have big plans for us?" Ben questions with a hint of sarcasm, lacing his every word with sarcasm.

"Well, I'll leave that up to you, Mr. Barnett." *I think I am so witty, with a large smile on* my face.

"Good, I'll pick you up at say 2?"

"Oh, um, I suppose, isn't 2 o'clock early for a date?" I ask.

"No. It's the perfect time. We will get there right on time," he says confidently.

"Okay, what do I need to wear? Is it formal, outdoorsy, or casual? Please tell me I am not meeting your parents." I shiver; I have not even met him as an adult yet.

"Kira, wear whatever you are comfortable in, no fancy dinner. You will see when I come to grab you."

"Okay, sounds good. I am pulling into my parents' house; I'll text you." I am still worried about what exactly we will be doing at 2 p.m. on a Saturday in June.

"Bye, Kira," he says teasingly. He knows I never say goodbye. So, with that, I hung up the phone and shut off my car. *chime* I look down in my hand at a text from Ben.

Ben 16:45 [RUDE.]

Kira 16:46 [You'll have to live with it for now; I'll get better about it!]

Ben 16:46 [We will work on it for sure.]

Kira 16:47 [No promises.]

With that, I head into the house, trying not to smile too much without looking like a weirdo. I walk into the house, set my stuff down, and see my parents' cooking dinner. By parents, I mean my mom, watching my dad cook on the peninsula with dark green granite. He has always been the family's cook; Mom can cook, but Dad enjoys it. I love it because he makes the best food ever.

She looks over, "Well, someone is in a good mood, huh?" she asks, knowing every expression I have ever made in my entire life.

"Why yes, Mum, I am. I have a date on Saturday," I say confidently, the confidence I do not feel at all when it comes to my Mom's relationship decisions.

"I did not realize you were talking to anyone or even dating. Kira, you have been home a month." She levels her gaze at me, "Don't rush into anything."

"Yes, Mother, I won't sleep with him on the first date." I roll my eyes and walk up to my dad, wrapping my arms around his belly while he is stirring something that smells too good on the stove.

He whispers, "Ignore her. I am just glad to see you smiling, bunny."

"Thank you, Daddy," I whisper into his back.

I head to change and walk Winston. Once we get outside, I take a few pictures of the landscape and crouch down to take a selfie with Win. I decided to post a few photos from the last few days; most recently, I took pictures of the books I have been reading and the food I've been eating. #bookish #foodie #dogmom #Mainesummers and post to my Instagram. I do not have a significant following. I only really have the friends I had in high school. There are also the people I have met throughout my Air Force career and the places I've lived.

Ding. I look down with excitement! To my surprise, it was not a text from Ben but a direct message from Penelope Nite. I remember her. We went to high school together; I used to be so jealous of how great her style was. She dressed so well for a teenager. While I was hanging around wearing camouflage and yoga pants to school, I had never heard of her called Penelope, only Penny. I wonder which she goes by now.

> Penny 17:00 [I was looking at your Instagram. We for sure read similar books. If you have any recommendations, please send them my way!]

> Kira 17:01 [Yes! Definitely! Text me; it will be easier to exchange recommendations, and we can chat about the ones we love!]

Oh my god! This is so exciting; I have not connected with anyone about the books I love to read before—most of the friendships I have to do with similar life experiences. Penelope, I hope you are ready for a new best friend!

After our walk, we headed into the house for dinner. We all eat in comfortable silence, and there are no more jabs on my personal life or questions about my day. Not only do

I have a date on Saturday, but I also have a potential new friend! Things are genuinely looking up.

I am startled awake by my alarm at 7 a.m. the following day. Thankfully, there were no nightmares this time. It's been a few days since the last nightmare with the odd resolution, and I haven't had another one. I don't know if I should be concerned or if my mind just needed time to settle after returning home. It's Friday; there is only one more day till my hot date with Ben. I go through my Instagram like I do every morning, and apparently, my Penny is a night owl. I click over to my messages.

Penny 22:30 [Hey, I am off tomorrow. Do you want to get coffee and look at books in town?]

Kira 07:05 [Good morning! Yes, of course! You name the time, and I'll be there.]

If I had stayed up that late, I would have been up at a different time than 7 a.m. I am going about my morning routine. I'm off work today, so I was going to lounge around the house. I got a good morning call from Ben asking how I slept and what I had planned for the day. Not knowing exactly what I had planned, I said he could call me after work, and I shouldn't be busy, but I couldn't make any promises.

Now, I'm sitting on the couch reading and daydreaming about Ben's lips, wondering how he would taste. I have been with a few men, and none have brought stars to my eyes or blown my mind. I am so embarrassed to think about it, but I have never truthfully gotten off by a man. I can fake it like the best of them, but the only thing to ever get me off is Joy, my purple vibrator. Her name is incredibly fitting because I always fall asleep after I spend time with Joy. Going to sleep smiling with no strings attached and no one to make me feel like shit about myself.

The characters in Sarah J Maas's books are just auspicious to have such attentive partners. Unfortunately, they are all fictional, which leads me to believe cumming from anything other than a battery-operated device will never happen. All the characters have been with their matches when they saw sparks and shattered utterly, so maybe I have never been with the right person. I'm rolling these thoughts around in my head when I get a notification from Penny.

Penny 10:00 [Hey, sorry! I was up super late reading. I just got up. Does 11 work for you?]

Kira 10:02 [I wish I could sleep like that! Yes, that sounds great. The bookstore in town?]

Penny 10:03 [Yes! See you then!]

Kira 10:04 [See you then!]

Chapter Six

Kira

I park my car in the back parking lot and make my way up the main street to the bookstore. Walking down any street, I feel like everyone is staring at me. Looking around I realize that I must be crazy. No one is looking at me; no one cares. Standing at the crosswalk, I step out. As I walked across, a car turned left toward where I was walking and did not see me. *See, stupid, no one.* I squeal and try to move out of the way; another car is coming now from the opposite direction. *BEEP* The other vehicle lays on the horn, catching the attention of the turning driver. She stops suddenly and barely 3 inches from my thigh. I let out a long breath, looking up at the vehicle that honked.

Benjamin Barnett is right in front of me in his truck. He pulls over into the open spot on the street and jumps out. Meeting me at the opposite end of the crosswalk, his gaze is thunderous. The furrow in his brow lurking under his ball cap. It was a tad menacing, but his eyes softened when he reached me, placing a hand on each shoulder. *They are green, oh my, he has green eyes flecked with brown. I immediately get warm, heat rising up my neck to my face. I must be so freaking red. Ben is holding you; you're staring into his eyes. SAY SOMETHING KIRA.* "Hi," It comes out breathless like I have not been breathing since he touched me.

"Jesus Christ, Kira, that scared the shit out of me. What was that woman thinking!?" He tries to keep his anger in check. The woman he's referring to is gone after our near miss.

"Oh, I don't know. I could have been in her blind spot, and there was an opening to go," I shrug, knowing I could have made the same mistake.

"Well, I still didn't like it. Are you really okay?" he says softly.

"Yes, I am even better now that you're here," I purred—*down girl.*

"Oh really," eyebrows raised, and the side of his lips curled up in a smile. Obviously, he can see what I am thinking in my eyes.

"Well, if I was going to meet up with you before our set date, I am glad you saved me. You have just achieved serious brownie points with my dad," I laugh.

"I am glad! Unfortunately, I do have to get back to the job site. I just ran to town for materials." He points his thumb over his shoulder to his still-running truck on the side of the road, loaded with boards. "But I'll call you tonight?" He asks, pleading in his expression.

"I am headed to my first girl date, ha-ha," I shrug, "But I'll text you when I get home."

"A... girl date?" His brow furrows again, and his voice drops to almost a grumble. *Is he jealous?* I think to myself.

"YES! I'm meeting a friend who loves books, too; we will have coffee and discuss them. It's a friend date, not a real date, ha-ha." I explained. "Why? Are you jealous?" I had to ask, wearing a knowing smile.

"No, I'm not... *ugh* I am not jealous." He mumbles.

"Okay, good. I'm all yours tomorrow." I smile. *Should we hug? Should I shake his hand for saving me, or maybe... Do it, Kira.* I step up onto my tiptoes, place my hand on his shoulder, and kiss his cheek as I pass him heading to the bookstore. He stiffens under my hand. "Talk to you tonight," I purr under my breath. *Do not look back… Be calm, be cool.*

***

Ben

Holy shit, a lot just happened in a matter of ten minutes. As Kira walks away toward the bookstore, I am glued to the spot. *She kissed me… She kissed me and just walked away.* I have not been this flustered in so long. I am warm all over, and I can feel the heat on my face. *I shake it off and make my way to the truck, lightly touching the cheek her lips were just on. They were just as soft as I thought they would be. I could feel her smile on my cheek. How the fuck am I supposed to focus on work now? This might be a bad idea, but I cannot wait to hold her in my arms tomorrow in my favorite place on the planet.*

***

Kira

As I walk through the doors to the bookshop with more confidence than I truly have, I spot her right away. Penelope Nite is about the same height as me. She has the most beautiful skin tone, as if the sun had naturally kissed her. With jet-black hair falling along her shoulders, she looks up, and her eyes light up, and she smiles. Almost running towards me, "Kira! It's so nice to see you!" She expressed with so much joy I could not help but smile.

"Hi! Penny, I was so excited and nervous to see you!" I cheer, "You will not believe what happened five minutes ago!" I insist.

"TELL ME!" Her eyes are wide and so ready for the juicy details. We make our way into the café side of the store and order our drinks. We sit down in the little set of tables and chairs. " Alright, spill," she demands.

"So, I was making my way over here; I parked in the back lot and had to cross the street," I say, "No one was coming,

I looked." I insist! "I am a quarter of the way through the crosswalk when a car comes pulling out right towards me," I whisper.

"What!? Did they not see you?" She gasps.

"I guess not. I was mid-squealing when someone honked their horn so loudly. It didn't just scare me but the lady who almost squished me into the pavement." I acknowledge. "I look up, and it is none other than the guy I met on a dating app that I am going on a date with tomorrow," I say sheepishly; I start to turn red all over again.

"Oh! A date! Well, that's one way to meet your future husband." She says with a little too much excitement.

"Who said anything about being my husband? We haven't even met as adults, let alone talked about what type of relationship we want." I hiss, growing redder and redder.

"Right, but wouldn't it be a great story to tell your children and grandchildren?!" She is whisper-yelling at me, trying to contain her excitement, eyes twinkling. She believes every word she is saying. "So… who is he?" She says with a curious smile.

"Well, umm." I hesitate. *Why am I so nervous about telling her?* "Benjamin Barnett," I say, rushed and still red. *Take a breath, Kira.*

"Oh man, I haven't seen him since high school. He was always so quiet." She says as if it's nothing, "What did you think? Is he the one?" She is being ridiculous now. But she might have it right.

"The one??? Um, I don't know about that. Although, I did something I have never done before in my entire life." I whisper, "I kissed his cheek and walked away. Didn't even look back; I came right to you." I clamped my mouth shut after the sentence rushed out of me. *I hope he does not hate me or isn't totally freaked out by the audacity of my behavior.* Penny stares at me, a massive smile growing on her lovely face.

"Oh man, you're going to drive him nuts." She says with confidence.

"What are you talking about, I just kissed his cheek. He saved my life. What else was I supposed to do?" I mumble out, looking down at the table.

"No, Kira. You kissed him to thank him, but then you walked away. You did not give him a chance to respond. He will probably think about that all night." She is laughing now, almost cackling.

"I'm glad my love life is so funny to you," I growled, with a scowl growing across my face. *She is still smiling at me with that evil grin.*

"I don't think it's funny at all; I think the situation is hilarious. Now let's talk about books," She switches the subject as if it's nothing. Probably noticing how uncomfortable I am. She knows exactly how to distract me from my thoughts. "Have you finished "A Court of Silver Flames" yet?" She asks all thoughts of Ben to dissolve from my mind.

"Oh man, I did this morning! It took me a while to read it, apparently… I am Nesta." I say resigned. "I had a lot of those issues after my divorce, not knowing who I was and not caring what people thought of me." I take a breath, "Now I just have to move into a house that takes care of me and helps me have sex with a massive, beautiful Illyrian who is already in love with me." I trail off, *thinking about what it would be like if Cassian, the Illyrian General, got down on his knees. Oh, my Kira, you are in public.* I look up; Penny is making the same face; I guess I am. Daydreaming about our fictional boyfriends like a best friend should.

"Oh, I'm sure you were nothing like Nesta; she could be so mean." She says with gentle eyes on me, "You are so kind; everyone goes through things. Life is hard, but we make it through. We do not give up, right?" Her eyebrows rise, "We just keep going down those stairs and lean on our friends when we need help." She did not realize how much I needed to hear that. *DO NOT CRY, KIRA! I'm going to cry;* my eyes well up with tears, and Penny does not bat an eye. She gets up, wraps her arms around me, and holds me close. "It's okay, Kira. We may only be new friends, but I'm not going anywhere," Penny whispers in my hair.

I sniffle loudly, "Thank you, Penny, that means so much to me." I hold back the gurgle stuck in the back of my throat from the snot building up from the tears, "I'm so glad you slid into my DM's; it meant the world." I have never said anything truer in my life.

"I would do it again in a heartbeat; now, let's dry these tears and go buy ourselves books." She exclaims, "Buying books makes everything better, right?"

"Oh yes! Let us do just that!" I whisper-shout. So, we did; we went through all the fantasy, romantic fantasy, rom-com, contemporary romance, and even the young adult sections. I got three because why not? I bought a book, a duplicate for Penny of the book I purchased so that we could read it together. We parted ways on our way out of the bookstore; more hugs, and I almost cried again, but I saved it for the car. Once there, I let out a big breath; a lot just happened. 1. I almost died, 2. I met Ben for the first time and kissed him, 3. Penny is the fucking bomb! I put the car into the drive and headed back home for the evening.

***

Ben

As I go home from the job site, my mind is constantly on Kira. *Why did she kiss me?* But more importantly, *why didn't she say anything*? I stay longer than usual and look down at the dash. 5:15 p.m. She quickly replied with a smiley face emoji, "Sounds good." With that settled, I pull into the driveway and get to work, letting Crash out. She has the zoomies, per usual, so I had to take her for a run as soon as I got home. Otherwise, there would be a mess on the floor.

She takes off after her ball, running and running and running like she has more energy than an energizer bunny. Once she has pooped and peed, we head back to the house; Crash has started carrying her food into the living room like she wants to eat next to me while I eat my grilled cheese sandwich and barbeque chips. "Crash, just eat at your bowl; I am right here," I growl because inevitably, she will not eat it all, and I will be stepping on crumbs for days. She does not listen and continues going back and forth, eating on the floor beside my feet. I roll my eyes and head for the shower.

Even here, I cannot seem to forget the touch of Kira's lips on my cheek. I grow even warmer under the constant stream of hot water. I can feel that kiss, small and delicate as it was, all the way down to my groin. I cover myself in soap and cannot help but touch myself. Rubbing my length to the thoughts of what other things Kira Logan could do to me with her soft, delicate lips. Her eyes are the deepest, darkest shade of blue I have ever seen. *Mmmm.* Just the thought of her eyes and mouth is enough to send me over the edge. I continue pumping myself until I see stars; I finally cum to thoughts of her dancing across my vision. This is not the first time I have done this thinking about her. Although it is my first time doing it, I know what her eyes look like in the flesh and how her lips feel against my skin.

A wave of exhaustion rolls through me as I finish cleaning myself and inevitably exit the shower. I towel off and walk back to my bedroom. Crash has crashed on the couch. I look at the alarm clock lighting up my nightstand in the dark. It was nearing 8, and I decide it was time to call her and find out what exactly that kiss was about.

Chapter Seven

Kira

I hear the chiming of my ringtone from my phone on the charge. I leap from my cozy spot in my reading chair. *It is fluffy and squishy, perfect for reading and passing out. If this chair were my boyfriend, we'd be married by now.* I think to myself as I make my way over to my phone. Answering "Hello" in a sing-song voice matches my mood, even after such a weird but fantastic day.

"Well, hello there," Ben rumbles into the phone. *God, could he have a sexier voice*? I think, "What are you doing tonight, pretty lady?" *Lord have mercy.*

"Oh, I was just reading in the most comfortable chair on the planet. How about you? What did you get into this evening?" I ask in the most teasing voice I can muster because I have been unable to get him off my mind. Everything that Penny said sounded wonderful. Imagine meeting in such a way and ending up married and completely in love.

"I worked late and finished a few things, so I wouldn't have to work tomorrow. Came home and did the usual." He says coolly, like nothing could fluster him the way I am constantly flustered during our conversations. Do I live rent-free in his head the way he lives in mine? I now know the color of his eyes up close, the feel of his hands on my shoulders, and his scent. I could get drunk off the smell of him; he was intoxicating in a way I had never felt before. I can't even describe the scent.

"Will you tell me our plans for tomorrow, or will I be kept waiting?" I say with a small amount of impatience. I wouldn't say I like surprises and never have will.

"No, but I will tell you we will be outside the entire time. So, pack sunblock and bug spray if you usually use it." He says it in a voice that shows me he is truly concerned like he is genuinely worried about me.

"I can pack whatever you'd like me to. Do you want me to bring anything else?" I ask hesitantly.

"No, just bring your beautiful self," he purrs. Everything inside me is burning; I am quite literally melting from the inside out. *Does he think I am beautiful?* I am questioning myself when I hear the rumble of his voice again.

"Wait, what? I missed that." I was utterly mortified. I was in my head, not listening to what he was saying.

"I was only asking why you walked away from me today after you kissed me," he pondered. "You did your no-goodbye thing; you do it every time, too."

"Ah, well, I was struggling with my confidence," I said, more truthfully than I thought I would be. "I was nervous that if I stopped walking or turned around, I wouldn't be able to stop at a kiss on the cheek," I whispered, feeling so immature.

He hums to himself, marinating on what I said, it seems. "If you had stopped and turned around to speak, I most likely would not have been able to stop you either." He goes quietly, waiting for me to respond.

"Oh," is the only word I can get out. *He feels it, too; he must.* I think to myself, there is a celebration going on in my head. *Focus Kira.!*

"Oh?" He asks. Did you think that I wasn't attracted to you, too?" He sounds exasperated. "You have been the only thing on my mind for the last few weeks. When your hand touched me, my body reacted when you kissed my cheek with your beautiful, soft lips." He growls low, rumbling through the phone. "It took everything inside me not to grab you right there in the street for the entire town to see."

I am panting; holy shit. "I… I had no idea…" I can't breathe, "I thought my touch angered you the way you went completely still. I thought I'd upset you. When you didn't call when you got home, I thought maybe… Maybe I ruined it." All my earlier confidence is gone; *I am self-sabotaging. Kira, he just told you he would jump you in the street, stop. You are worth love.* I coach myself out of the shell I pull back into during times like these. All my insecurity envelopes me and does not allow me to let anyone in.

"Kira, it was the exact opposite." He interrupts my mind spin, "I was worried I'd scare you with my reaction. I was so worried you'd get hurt; I was so worried I wouldn't get to hold you even for the first time." He whispers, "That woman could have killed you or severely injured you, and I haven't even gotten to taste your lips on mine." He breathes deeply into the receiver. *I wish we were having this conversation in person because I would do it; I would kiss him right here. I wonder if he masturbates as much as I do.* The intrusive thought hits me. *Maybe it will break this incredible tension happening.*

"Will you Facetime me?" I ask, expecting the answer to be no.

"Yes." He insisted, "Doing it now."

The call waiting sound chimes in my ear; I pull the phone away and hit the green circle. I allowed him to see me in my pajamas with my hair in a half-up mess. I'm wearing my big blue before-bed glasses. *It's fine; if he likes you, he will like this side of you, too.* I can almost hear Penny whispering into my ear as I let the self-consciousness go and look at the beautiful man looking back at me. I can see the awkwardness in his face as he looks back at me, eyes hooded and a slight smirk hitching up a corner of his kissable lips.

"Hi there," I say, even though we've been talking for a little while already. He is wearing a red Nike shirt; his hat is off. *I don't think I have ever seen him with his hat off before. He needs a haircut, but the relaxed, mussed hair really is doing it for me. And oh my, that beard. I can just imagine the things he could do to torture me with that. Kira, you're ogling.*

Say something. "Well, it's nice to meet you face to face on Facetime." I giggle, and a smile crosses my face.

"Hello to you too. You have the most beautiful smile, Kira. I am sure you've heard it before, but it is enchanting." He says calmly, coolly, and finally relaxed. Seeing me was all he needed to release that built-up tension. "What would you like to talk about tonight?" He asks.

"Well, Benjamin Barnett, what is your favorite color?" I tease.

He lifts a brow with a face that could only say, "Hmmm, there are so many good ones, but I will go with red." "What about you, Kira Logan? What is your favorite color?" Ben asks; it's all business now.

"Purple, but you need to choose another question. That one was mine." I say in my sassiest voice.

"No need to be sassy; purple is a less nice color, by the way." I shoot him a glare. " Do you have a favorite number? If so, why?" he asks.

"I do have a favorite number; it doesn't have some huge meaning behind it, but it's 14. It was my student number growing up and I always somehow ended up with it. Also, I love 7, 21, 28."

"Hmm, interesting; you just love all the divisions of 7, then?" He responds quickly.

"Yes and no, I only like the first 4." "Do you have a favorite number? And why?" I question, without looking away from his intent-filled stare.

"2, but I don't have a hidden meaning. I think it's just lucky." I let out a massive yawn after this response. "Am I boring you lady?" He teased. *Did he call me lady?!*

"Excuse me, Lady?" I ask pointedly. "And for your information, no, I am tired!"

"Lady, it is what you are, correct?" He says there is no issue with the pet name he gave me. I am tired, too. Maybe we can save the rest of these questions for tomorrow's date." The smile that fills his entire face is magnificent. His eyes crinkle at the edges while his eyes almost twinkle. His expression is delighted, as if he is excited to see me.

"Yes, let's save the rest for tomorrow." I whisper, "Thank you for Facetiming with me; it means a lot." I'm being shy now for some ridiculous reason. "Sweet dreams, handsome," I say with a small amount of confidence in my tone.

"Goodnight, beautiful. I'll see you at 2., but I'll call you in the morning." He smiles once more and disappears from the screen. He didn't let me say goodbye this time, and I could not believe him. He gives me so much shit about not saying goodbye, and he hangs up. *WHAT THE FUCK.* It's all I can think of as I pull up our message change and give him a small piece of my mind.

> Kira 21:35 [Excuse me! For someone who always wants to say goodbye, that wasn't nice!]

> Ben 21:37 [Doesn't taste good, does it?]

Does what taste good?? I think to myself as I type my subsequent text to Ben.

> Kira 21:39 [Taste?]

> Ben 21:39 [Yes, of your medicine lady. Not very nice, huh?]

REALLY! I think, what a turkey. Oh, bickering with this man is going to be wonderful. As I type the last text of the night, I pass out immediately after I hit send. Falling asleep with the biggest smile, my mind is filled with thoughts of his mouth, eyes, and touch. *Oh, Kira, you are in so much trouble.*

Kira 21:40 [Goodnight, handsome]

Ben 21:40 [Good night, beautiful]

Chapter Eight

Kira

Today is the day. I wake up early because I am too excited to see what Ben has planned for us. I have showered, washed everything, shaved everything. *You never know what could happen.* I may have told my mom I wouldn't have sex on the first date, but all the best relationships start with a chemistry test. What's more fun than the ultimate test of whether we are truly compatible? I have been pacing around all day; Ben called this morning to ensure I slept well. He is so sweet about that after I told him about that terrible nightmare and its subsequent final one.

Since the call, I've been buzzing, pulling everything out of my closet. I started with a yellow sun dress but switched to jean shorts and a pretty blouse. That was too casual. After trying on a few more outfits, I returned to the yellow sun dress. The dress is bright with a sweetheart neckline, and the skirt lands just above my knee; finishing off the outfit with my favorite maroon Vans slide-on sneakers and some soft waves in my shoulder-length blonde hair. I am ready.

***

Ben

I am on my way to pick up Kira; I have been nervous and excited all at once for the entire day. I used my push mower to mow the path down the trail to my favorite spot. After that, I was drenched in sweat. I ended up hoping in the shower. I got all cleaned up and dressed; I headed to the grocery store to get the last items I needed for the picnic. From talking to her, I have come to find out she loves ham and provolone cheese subs, barbeque chips, and red grapes. Once I get home, I arrange the picnic basket so it is ready to go when we get back here.

The house I live in isn't anything to write about, but it is a roof over my head till I find a way to tear it down and rebuild it. The house sits on two acres. What I wasn't told when I bought the property was that there is a small pond toward the back with a huge willow tree. The tree has large branches that are perfect for a swing. When I had the time, I created a sizeable rope-hung wood plank swing. I have never brought anyone back here; it is my happy place. I hope Kira Logan appreciates it as much as I do. I loaded the truck and headed over to her house. She still lives in the same house she grew up in; her parents have added onto it and remodeled it from head to toe throughout the years she has been gone. She told me they didn't change her bedroom much, so it still felt like home whenever she visited.

As I pull up to her house, she waits outside on the porch with a black lab at her side. She reads a book when she looks up; her parents don't seem home. Only her four-runner is here. She lifts her hand and waves, standing and letting Win greet me before we head off. He is a beautiful dog, calm with eyes that could put Crash's to shame. "Hey Ben, just a minute, let me get him in the house and grab my purse." She looks absolutely beautiful. Yellow is not my favorite color, but it makes her glow. *You are in so much trouble*, I think to myself.

"Hi Kira, that's fine. I'll wait for you right here." My eyes roamed from her honey-blond hair to her sexy legs. I coughed, our eyes met, and she blew me a kiss before heading through the door. *Yep, serious trouble.*

***

Kira

Back in the house, I get Winston settled with a bone and ensure he has water and food. My parents went house hunting even though they did not need a new home. Whatever floats their boat is fine with me. With a kiss on his handsome snout, I headed to Ben's truck. *Gods, did he look dreamy?* I think that as I make my way to the passenger side, Ben does the gentlemanly thing and opens the door for me. "Big step," Ben whispers.

"Thank you, that is very kind of you," I say, cheeks on fire. No one has ever opened a door for me once, and I am at a loss for words.

"Not a problem, beautiful," he purrs. *My god, I am on fire, calm down Kira. This is a first date; be reasonable. I* think while I watch him walk around the truck and climb in. He adjusts his seat and pulls the truck onto the road. The windows are down on this gorgeous day. He lives about fifteen minutes from my parents' house, we pull into the driveway. A tiny white house with black trim is tucked away from the road. There is a two-car garage, but he parks in front of them, not inside. "Wait here," he says while he slips out of the truck and makes his way around the truck to open my door.

My face is red again as he opens the door and takes my hand. He never takes his eyes off me, watching me. Every expression I make as I take in the property is quiet and calm here. This is a quiet road, and there is undeveloped land. "Ben, this place is so lovely; what do you have planned for us?" I ask carefully. I have a feeling he will not tell me until we get there.

"Are you ready to start our date?" his eyebrows raise in challenge.

"Oh, I thought it started when you picked me up at my house?" I counter with another raised eyebrow back at him.

"It did," he teased. He reaches out and grabs my hand. He pulls me up to the walkway around his house with a tug.

A basket and a backpack are waiting for him there. Once we reach the supplies, he releases my hand for only a moment, placing the backpack on his back and lifting the basket with his other hand. We turn toward the wood line; a mowed line runs straight through the backyard. It stops at the wood line with an opening in a field stone rock wall. Walking down the trail, I notice so much; I take everything around me. The smells, the sounds, and all the green surrounded me.

The trail is lined with towering Eastern White Pine trees, one of the trees Maine is known for, and the common Red Oak trees. The Red Oak trees are enormous; where the pine trees towered growing straight up, the oaks grow upward, and their branches grow outward. Small birds jump from limb to limb, and squirrels gather and forage around us. I feel Ben's gaze on me and look up; his hazel eyes with flecks of brown are sparkling. "You look beautiful today, Kira," he confided with a slight smirk.

My cheeks heat as I tuck my chin to my chest, "Thank you." I am still at a loss for words; it has been so long since I have been in the woods of Maine, and this grove is stunning. "You look incredibly handsome yourself, Mr. Barnett." I wink. A look moves across his face, his eyes dilate, and they disappear as quickly as they arrive. *Desire,* that's all I can think of. *Be good, Kira.*

"We're almost there," he says with hooded eyes and a low rumble of his voice that goes directly between my thighs. I looked up; there was a shining twinkle in the distance. *Is that,* I think, looking over at Ben, who is grinning down at me?

"Is that a pond? Oh god, is that a willow tree?" I ask with glee. I bounce. Willows are my absolute favorite tree of all time."

"It is a willow; I made a swing for it if you'd like a ride." His face goes red as he, too, hears the innuendo in his voice.

My face flushes red as I tell him, "Oh yes, please," with more confidence than I genuinely possess—*down girl.* We make our way over to the tree, where Ben sets down our supplies and shows me to the swing. He helps me get on, making sure I am steady, for he steps behind me and gives me a gentle push once, twice, a third time. He moves to the tree trunk, watching me intently as I pump my legs and fly through the air. It is breathtaking out here, and the pond twinkles in the sunlight almost magically. The constant sea breeze from the coast makes the thin hanging branches and leaves sway in the breeze. I genuinely feel like I am in a

Mary Balogh story, falling madly in love with the duke who has no business being with a person of my status. I would not be any nobility in that world, but Benjamin Barnett would, devilishly handsome and so quiet. If only he knew my feelings and wants for him since he saved my life in town.

****

Ben

After touching her back on the swing, my hands are buzzing. I watch her while I lean on this tree. I want to rip her off the swing. Lay her down on our blanket and make sweet love to her. She looks stunning, floating through the air in the place I love most. She loves it. She notices me watching her and starts to slow herself. I have not moved; I cannot. *Breathe Ben.* Her eyes have not left mine; she is walking towards me. I do not remove my hands from my pockets as she gets nearer and nearer. She stops in front of me; there is one foot between us, and her chest is heaving with large breaths. Mine did the same, our hearts pounding in unison.

Kira lifts her hand to my face, tracing her fingers along my beard and back down to my neck. My heart will fly out of my chest; the desire to grab her is almost unbearable. She lifts herself on her toes, resting her palms on my chest, eyes falling closed; she kisses me. A tentative, soft, delicious kiss. She moans into my mouth, and I am lost in her smell, wrapping my hands around her waist. I explore her entire body with my hands; her arms climb up to around my neck. She pulls me in closer like she cannot get enough.

***

Kira

I am drowning; my god, he smells so good. His lips are so soft and rough simultaneously; his beard tickles the edges of my mouth most deliciously. His hands were large, warm, and strong, roving over my entire body. I am drenched for him; my underwear is useless. His hands move over my ass and down my thighs; as they climb back up, they descend under my dress. Pulling my thigh up to his waist, I lean into him; I can feel his hard length against me. Exactly where I need him, his hands continue to wander. Our mouths fused, tasting and biting. Only separating to take gulping breaths, his hands dive into my lace thong. I gasp when his finger moves through my folds, finding that spot that drives me wild. He growls in a way that promises more, "I want all of you," he whispers in my hair.

"You can have it; please don't stop," I manage to rasp out between kisses.

"Are you sure," He questions.

"Yes, please, do whatever you want to me. Just don't stop." I am grabbing him everywhere; I have no idea what to do with my hands. My brain is fuzzy, and I wait for him to take me. He lifts me and carries me over to our things. He gently sets me down on my feet, drops to his knees, and rips open the backpack. Grabbing the blanket inside, he lays it beneath the willow. I feel cold without the press of his body on me as I am buzzing with anticipation. *Breathe, Kira, it's okay; you are fine. Let yourself be happy; let yourself be free.* I say to myself, trying to calm my anxiety. *We will not be telling Mom about this part of the day.* I laugh to myself quietly.

Ben looks up at me questioningly before I sit on the blanket. He settles down next to me. Leaning in, he places his large, warm, rough hands on my cheek and pulls me in for a kiss. Tasting me with that delicious tongue, his mountain and woody smell is intoxicating. I lean into the kiss more; he pulls back and places a finger on my lips.

Moving down my body with kisses on my neck, along my dress, and finally kneeling before me, he kisses my thighs lightly. Teasing me in a way that makes me squirm, I have never had a man so eager to taste me. "You are so fucking beautiful, Kira," he growls out as he's kissing deeper down my legs. I lay back, waiting for what's next; he slides his hands up my thighs, removing the drenched scrap of fabric covering my wetness. He lifts it to his nose and takes a deep breath, "You smell fucking incredible." He breathes, eyes completely dilated, looking feral. Laying down on his stomach, he dives between my legs, tasting every inch of me. Licking my folds, swirling around my clit like he cannot get enough. He slides a finger inside, and I buck; I begin to feel warmth swirling at the back of my spine. Fingering me within an inch of my life, I can't breathe. *I am going to cum holy shit,* I think.

"Ben," I gasp out.

"HMMMM," he hums a response. Inserting another finger inside my already quivering sex.

"I am going to…. I am going to cum." I am on the verge of screaming. My eyes slammed closed, I saw stars, and my world began to shatter. With one more flick of his tongue over my clit while fingering me at the same time, I crest. Falling off the edge of my orgasm, I cannot breathe. My chest heaving, Ben slowly sits up and climbs over me. Leaning into me, he kisses me; I can taste myself on him; his mouth is coated in my taste. *My god, I think I have died and gone to heaven.* Ben doesn't waste time; he leans back, pulling his shirt over his head, unbuckling his pants.

"Do you want me, Kira?" he asks with such gruffness I almost come apart again right here. I am shaking my head up and down quickly; standing, I lift my dress over my head, standing on the blanket in a strapless bra that is very skewed already, and vans slide on sneakers. Ben lays down on his back, leaning toward his jeans to grab a condom. *Good, he came prepared; I guess my shaving and washing wasn't a waste of time.* I think as I watch him rip the wrapper with his tear, taking care to remove it. He pumps himself a few times and places the condom on; it's erotic to watch him roll it on.

I kick off my shoes, unhook my bra, and step over him. As I straddle his legs, he grabs ahold of my hips and guides me down to him. Once I am fully seated on his cock down to the hilt, he reaches up and kisses me. A gentle, loving kiss that takes my breath away.

Catching my breath, enjoying every inch of him inside me, I whisper, "I never do this." He raises an eyebrow in response. "I never just have sex with someone on a first date; I just, I couldn't help myself." *Shut up, Kira, live in this moment.* He silences me with more kisses; he knows and doesn't care. He's here for it and wants me. *Enjoy Kira, fuck his brains out.* I start to move on top of him. I was clenching and unclenching myself around his hard dick. He feels so fucking incredible.

"It has been a while; this may not take long, but I want you to cum again, Kira. Will you cum for me?" He rasps, trying to hold his composure. I nod in response as I continue moving up and down on him. Rubbing my breasts across his chest, he reaches his hand between and starts to make circles around my clit. My body reacts as tingles spread through my body. I can't think. I toss my head back, unable to keep the moan inside as he works me. Stars sparkle through my vision as I climb and climb; the orgasm almost has me. "Cum for me, Kira," he growls, rumbling through my entire body. With just those words, I am cresting and falling off the cliff.

"Oh my god, Ben, I am... I am cumming," I whisper-scream, unable to control my volume, as I begin to moan into him. With the sound and feel of my orgasm, Ben grabs me in response. Fucking up into me over and over until his hips rise one final time, and he lets out a roaring moan that is the hottest thing I have ever fucking seen. While cumming and twitching beneath me, he reaches up and pulls me down to him.

Holding me tight, he kisses the top of my head in the most gentle and tender way. I can't move; I refuse to get up. I am so warm and cozy in his embrace. We lay under the willow, feeling the sea breeze cooling our sweat-covered skin. A shiver runs down my back, and Ben pulls me closer.

"Are you alright, Kira?" Ben asks quietly into my hair. While slowly rubbing his hands up and down my back.

"I am fantastic," I breathe into him. "How are you?"

He chuckles, "I promise I didn't plan that, but since you kissed my cheek, I haven't been able to get you out of my mind." He takes a breath, "I am wonderful. Are you hungry?" He looks up at me and smiles with a beautiful, toothy grin.

"Starved!" With that, we put our clothes back on and ate the picnic—my favorite sandwich and chips; he brought Coke Zero, my secret guilty pleasure. It is his as well. I think he checked every box as we ate in comfortable silence. Once we had finished eating, we talked about small stuff, little questions, nothing serious. We were content just relaxing together by the pond and just being together.

Chapter Nine

Kira

Lying there in bed with Winston tucked in close to me, all I can think about is Ben. I have never experienced that kind of draw between someone else or this chemistry. He made me feel seen more than I ever have in my life. I felt as though I was the only girl in the world. I am by no means the most petite girl; I have some soft curves and could lose ten or fifteen pounds, but he looked at me like I was a million bucks.

When I was swinging through the branches of the willow tree, looking back at Benjamin, he had his hands tucked deep in his pockets and eyes locked on me. His gaze could have melted tungsten; the desire in his eyes was unmistakable. I slowed my swing and took the chance, giving in to the desire I had felt since the first time I touched him. I have genuinely never felt a pull to someone before in my life. He smells like the mountains, woods, and freedom. His lips felt warm and spectacularly luscious, and the kiss was gentle but firm—a promise for more and oh so much more.

I dive into the memory of how he devoured me like I was his last meal, he savored and reveled in the taste of me. He would not let me return the favor this time, but I will taste him. After he had his fill of me, he took me on the blanket beneath the willow, and I have relived every exceptionally passionate moment over and over. I will fall asleep tonight with thoughts of more: what would life be like with Benjamin Barnett? Would this desire fade, or would we continue to want in abundance for the rest of our lives? *Gods, I hope so; I hope that I am enough; I hope I can fill this hole inside myself with him.* I think as I drift off to sleep.

* * *

Ben

I am in so much trouble. I thought if I got a taste of her, I could get her out of my head. Instead, all I can think about is her constantly. Her taste, smell, eyes, touch, everything that makes Kira, Kira. Her eyes are like the deepest parts of the ocean. A never-ending dark blue in which you could inevitably drown. I am drowning in Kira everywhere. I can still smell her on the blanket I laid beneath the willow tree. As I lay here tonight, my mind raced with thoughts of her. I fall asleep to the sound of her laugh in my head and the scrunch of her nose when she smiles. *I am fucked. I may already be in love with a girl I have met twice since we were 18 years old.* I think as I begin to drift deeper into sleep.

***

Kira

It's Monday. I have talked to Ben daily; we have even planned to hang out after work tomorrow evening. I promised to make my chicken paprika. I made it for dinner the night we had our first phone call. I have a full day of work and a half day tomorrow. I finish getting ready for work and run out to my four-runner. On Mondays, my parents are both off so that they can explore together. In the car, my phone starts to chime the familiar ring I have set up for Ollie, "Hello, Ollie, what's up?" I ask, confused, why he was calling me at 8 a.m. on a Monday.

"Hey, Kira. I was reading the newspaper." He says hesitantly, almost not wanting to tell me this story.

"And?" I am baffled.

"Yeah, so it says here that Avery Lark died a little over a week ago." He goes incredibly quiet.

"I am not hearing this correctly; did you say Avery died in the last two weeks?" *It cannot be; he could not have happened the same night he apologized.* I think, God, I am reeling from the news. "Are they sure?"

Ollie is quiet for a minute, "Yes, he went overboard in the Bering Sea, and it took them over a week to find his body washed up on the Alaskan coast." He says, "Are you okay? I know you have a no-contact order, but you seem more frazzled about this than I expected." *True, I am sure he thought I'd be jumping for joy or singing hallelujah.* But no one deserves to die. Especially like that, no wonder he was so weird and troubled in my dream. No wonder he disappeared so abruptly. "Kira, are you there?" he asks, sounding exasperated.

"Yes, yes, Ollie, I'm here. Thank you for telling me. I'm sorry it has just been a weird few weeks." I say with a voice that sounds foreign to my ears. "I, uhm, just got to work. I will call you later today or tomorrow. Then we can talk. I love you."

"I love you, Kira. You deserve so much more than what he gave you." Ollie says with hate in his voice. *If he only knew half of it,* I think because I did not tell my family even that. I hang up the phone because that is what I do; Ollie knows and doesn't get offended. He understands me, mostly. I lied to him, though I was not at work yet, and to tell you the truth, I don't even know if I can go in. How do I reconcile what I am feeling? I have been over Avery for a decade; I have… I had a restraining order against him and no contact, but I saw him. That had to have been real, right?

I go through the dream sequence in my head, well the main portions I remember. *He was there, he grabbed me, he was his scary ass self that I remember, but this time I got away, I got away, but I turned around and went back. I returned to the lion's den, where I knew danger was because I had to know. He was crying, he was apologizing, and then what? He was gone.* I think to myself. Avery Lark is gone. I never have to wonder anymore or feel uneasy; I know now from a lot of therapy that I am enough. But it is almost bittersweet because he did not get to hear or see how fucking fantastic I am. *Grief is a weird thing; I know that it comes in waves, but I never thought that I'd even grieve my ex-husband in my lifetime or that I would feel anything.* I thought to myself, *for sure, he would live to be 1,000 because he was the devil, but in reality, he was just human like all of us.*

Chapter Ten

Ben

I spent the entire weekend working around the property, cleaning, doing oil changes on equipment, and talking to Kira. We text all day and have our good morning and good night calls every day. It's Monday now, and I have been up since 4:30 doing my regular work routine. Paperwork, coffee, and thinking about Kira. We have a date here at the house tomorrow night; she promised to make me her "famous chicken paprika." *I am skeptical, first because I've never had it and second because I only cook for myself, which isn't usually fancy: spaghetti and meatballs, chicken tenders, pizza, meatloaf, etc. The classics for a growing boy like me. I look forward to seeing her and kissing her and anything else she will let me do to her.*

It's about 8:30. when I get a text message from Kira. *That's odd. I just talked to her, and she was excited to see me.* I think to myself, I read.

> Kira 08:30 [Hey Ben, I'm not sure I can hang out tomorrow. Something has happened, and I am not ready to talk about it yet.]

Well, what the heck? I don't usually get this disappointed about being blown off, but this is a little irritating. *You're fine, Ben. Something has come up, she still might change her mind about hanging out, and you don't need to sit and overthink. You have had your issues and things that come up in the past, and you can also be patient with her. This may end up being nothing...* I tell myself because it's true; I was just surprised.

> Ben 08:30 [Oh no. Is everything okay?]

> Kira 08:32 [Yes, something personal came up... I just don't think I am ready to share just yet. I'm sorry.]

> Ben 08:32 [Okay, whatever you need. Could you call me later tonight? I'm here if you need me.]

> Kira 08:33 [Yes, I'll call you tonight.]

With a bit of disappointment still rolling through me, I will have to see what's going on with her and see if I can do anything to fix it. I hope it wasn't what we did the other night, I think to myself. She has become something I never honestly expected to find in this world.

***

Kira

I don't know why I am backing out of the date with Ben; I need time to figure out all these feelings. It is something when a person that you thought you felt safe with was an absolute psychopath inside and out. Your mind thinks that you would have such a profound reaction even after you have not seen them in almost ten years. This is not the grief I am feeling but relief. Relief that even though that pain, suffering, and self-doubt were all never going to happen again, not by his hand and no other man. With this feeling, my brain is trying to protect me. *I know Benjamin would never harm me. I also thought about Avery and looked where that got me. For goodness's sake, I had sex with him on our first date. I don't regret it, but are we moving too fast? Do I take time to think about things before our date on Tuesday? Or should I reschedule altogether?*

I called out of work and decided today was not my day to be strong. I will stay home and have a me day. After a call to my therapist, she said she had an open slot for 12:30.

As I dial into my appointment, I think of Ben. Should I talk to her about him as well? She will not judge me but give me that unbiased opinion I need. Julie has been my rock for the last few years and has helped me through many issues. She has shown me that I am not only what others put into me; my worth lies within myself. I never need to measure my self-worth against anyone else's. If people do not like me, that is their problem, not mine. I still suffer from being a people pleaser and worrying about what others think of me, but we cannot fix everything about ourselves overnight.

"Hi Kira, are you okay? We haven't had a last-minute appointment in a long time," Julie says with a softness in her voice that immediately brings me peace.

"Oh Julie, the most insane things have been happening over the last few weeks, and well, today was kind of the straw that broke the camel's back." I rush out in one breath.

"Okay, let's start from the beginning, then. What has been happening, and is there a root cause that we know of, or do you need help discovering it?"

"I started having nightmares again," I saw hesitantly. I heard Julie hmmm into the phone. "They are about Avery again, but this time, they were different."

"Different, how?" She asks calmly.

I take a deep breath, count to four in my head, and begin. I told her about how the dreams started in our first apartment, how I could smell and see everything, but there wasn't a lot I could do. Before anything else could happen, I'd wake up. I told her that in the last dream, I could get away, but I went back.

"How odd. Why do you think you went back into the apartment?" she asks in a confused tone.

"Well, I thought he'd chase me. Make me come back like every other time I could get out of his grip in real life." Taking a breath, I say, "But it was different, Julie. Something felt off. I went back in, and he was sobbing in the main bedroom. He was apologizing over and over and told me I deserved better." I try my best to explain.

"Okay. Have you spoken to or seen him since you have been home?" she speculated.

"No, he doesn't even live in the area. None of his family is here either." I explain, "That's the weird part, he died."

"When?" She sounded as surprised as me when I first heard.

"He fell overboard, and it took them quite a while to find him; he washed up in Alaska yesterday, which means around the time of my last dream, he was either dying or had already died." I breathe out, *unsure why I struggle to talk about this.*

"Well, that is intriguing. So, in a way, you knew he died without knowing he died and are now processing that fact that your brain was correct—that maybe he was visiting you in a dream state." Julie reasons, "We know you've had déjà vu dreams that end up coming true. Maybe that's what has happened here?" She questions.

"That's the thing. I don't understand why it happened in the first place and why I am reacting this way. I should be jumping for joy, but it feels like grief. It shouldn't be grief." I am holding back tears.

"Kira, you're an empath. You feel more than an average person does; you may have hated him entirely, but a person died. A person who was in your life for a few years and left a large mark on your soul, heart, and body." She reconciles, "You cannot expect to have no emotions at all for the death of a person; if you don't feel anything at all, then that's when something should be wrong." Julie says, "You are human; you are allowed to feel, and these emotions may feel weird and unhelpful. You can only learn to deal with them."

I sit quietly, thinking about her words. Since it happened, I finally found the confidence to tell her what I had wanted to say. I tried to call her and scream from the rooftops that I had found someone who could be my person for life. "Julie, there's something else," I say, trying to hide the happiness in my tone.

"Oh really, you sound like you're smiling." She interjects.

Well, I tried to hide the happiness. "I met someone. He is everything, and I might have had sex with him on our first date." I say far too quickly, but I know she speaks Kira.

"Kira! That's so exciting. I know we've talked about you taking your time, but I told you if it feels right, you don't have to hold back." She says, "Tell me about him. How did you meet? That date must have been something to get you to that point." I can hear the sarcasm lacing her tone.

"He and I went to high school together; we never really spoke, and our paths only crossed in the lunchroom and hallways." I disclose, "We met on that new dating app with the female message first. He came up, and I just got a zing. I would thoroughly regret it if I didn't swipe right or message him." I continue, "He is kind, attentive, smart, hardworking, and most of all, he makes me feel seen." I detail what happened and how everything is going now and ask, "Do I meet up with him on Tuesday or give whatever I am feeling some time?"

"Kira, you need to be honest with Benjamin about what is going on in your life. You trusted him enough to tell him about the dreams. Now, you must trust enough to tell him how you feel and that this changes nothing between you." She explains gently, "You have not had anyone this close to your heart in a long time; he sounds perfect for your needs. It's okay to open up to him, but if you're uncomfortable, that is okay too. Just be honest, whatever you decide." She concludes. We hung up because we were out of time; I wish she were more than my therapist. I need a girlfriend to talk to about these things; that's when I think, *Penny!*

Chapter Eleven

Kira

Kira 13:10 [Hey Penny, are you busy today?]

Penny 13:12 [Not today! I have the day off, what's up?]

Kira 13:13 [I have a lot on my mind and want to see you and talk. Anything and everything, also buy books.]

Penny 13:14 [I am here whenever you need me! What time would you like to meet at the cafe?]

Kira 13:15 [Does 2 p.m. work for you?]

Penny 13:16 [2 p.m. works perfect, see you soon.]

With that, I get myself together and finally shower for the day. Get dressed and look human again, with Winston following me around the house. He can't seem to shake the fact that I am upset, and he isn't sure what's going on. He has always known when something is wrong, but I feel off even if something isn't bad. So, he is following me for now, placing his sweet head in my lap whenever I sit down. He looks up at me with those eyes that ground me and make me remember that no matter what, I am loved. He has been and will always be here for me. *He will never die; he can't.* I think to myself as I look down at him.

I walk into the bookstore café and see Penny has already ordered our coffee and got us chocolate chip cookies. She sees me and hops out of her chair, "Kira!" She embraces me in a big hug that makes me never want to let go. I'm not sure why I want to cry, but I do; I want my new friend to comfort me and help me figure out my life. My talk with Julie was not long enough, and I'm sure this chat won't be long either, but it feels good to talk about things.

I have always thought that if you can get to a point where the words come out, they don't cause pain, and it gets better. There was a time in my life when I told no one what had been happening to me, around me, and within me. Now, I will tell anyone who asks I am an open book because words are just that. Words, if directed at someone in a hostile way, hurt, but talking about what is causing pain will sting at first, then slowly, over time, you build up almost a tolerance for it, which I think is the actual healing.

"Penny, oh gosh, you didn't have to get my drink and cookies." I am practically drooling and looking at them. "Let's sit. I need to vent and get your opinion," I say quietly.

"Okay, what's going on? Are you okay? Did things not go well with Ben? You sounded so happy after I talked to you Sunday." She discloses.

"Well, I had been having nightmares about my ex-husband a few weeks ago; it turns out he died around the time of the nightmares," I explain; she sucks in a breath because death is terrible doesn't matter who it happens to.

"You saw him in your dreams, and then he died? That's insane; no wonder you're feeling so weird. When did you find out? She asks with so much empathy and love in her eyes.

"I found out this morning. I'm trying to figure out why I care and am so upset. I canceled plans with Ben, and he may hate me." As I explain every detail of the last few weeks, my eyes are welling up with tears. Penny, God bless her, listens with rapt attention to every detail, trying to mask how she's feeling so I don't spiral again. Once I am finished telling her everything, I ask what I should do now: do I tell Ben, or do I just let it go?

"Kira, we don't know each other super well yet, but I feel like I have known you my whole life. You are genuine, caring, smart, and, if I'm frank, a smoke show. We both know you like him; you slept with him. He rocked your world and is easy for you to open up to. If you explain as you have to me, he will understand. Mind you, I don't know all the sordid details of what happened all those years ago; I am sure you don't need to go into that because, well, I think it will warp his perspective. I wonder why such a monster deserves your empathy, but Kira, you are an emotional person. Ben would be stupid not to see it for what it is." She explains calmly, "Someone died, someone you used to know. It probably has you thinking about what could happen to you, and you're scared."

"I guess I didn't think of it that way. And thank you for those lovely compliments… If I look at it as if I only knew Avery as a name, I would have felt sympathy and empathy, sure, but I would also worry about what it would be like for everyone I love if I died so suddenly at 28 years old." My voice and face cleared of the emotions welling up. "It's not that it's Avery; it's just me." I declare, feeling a teensy bit better about the whole thing.

"Yes! Exactly; also, you can't let Ben go even for a night." Her eyes are sparkling as she teases me, "That is one handsome man, and he seems to be incredibly taken with you; he didn't say much in school to anyone; he kept his head down and got his work done, but he's completely different from you. I doubt he's even an ounce mad; if anything, he is probably just worried about you." She insists, standing up and wrapping me in another hug. "Now, let's go get some books!"

"Yes, please... And thank you, Penny, I needed to hear all that." I whisper into her hair, not ready to let go of her warmth and happiness in this embrace. "You have made coming home to Hamlin that much easier..."

***

Ben

It has been such a long day; I have been distracted the entire time. Worrying about Kira and what could have spooked her in such a way. We finish the next task on our long list of items needed for the Dodd project; Dick Dodd is starting to become a little frustrating. He has added a few more things that aren't quite in the scope of work for which we had a contract. We discussed a price for the additional work, and he was okay with the cost. These further changes are going to push back the completion timeline. The building is coming together beautifully, though; the house is framed, the roof is on, and the windows are in. We will hopefully be wrapping up the outside while the plumbers and electricians are hard at work roughing in.

It's about 2 p.m. when I hear my phone *ping*.

Kira 14:07 [Hey! I am so sorry about earlier; we are still good for Tuesday. I'll call you this evening and fill you in. Sometimes, I jump the gun on things before I have the time to calm down.]

Kira 14:07 [Also, it has nothing to do with you. You have been amazing, I promise.]

I was thinking about her, I think as I respond to the text.

Ben 14:08 [Oh, Hun, that's okay. You had me worried there that something had happened or you would be hurt somehow.]

Ben 14:08 [As long as you're okay, we're okay. I look forward to the call. Enjoy the rest of your day!]

Kira 14:10 [You too! Sorry again. It means a lot that you were worried about me, though. I've never had that outside of my family. Talk to you soon, Ben.]

Ben 14:11 [Sounds good, bye Kira]

After finally hearing from her, I feel I can go about my day; she will tell me what's happening. Finishing up the last bit of window trim for the day, I get into a groove, and the guys pay attention to their tasks. It's beautiful down on the coast; it is a hard place to work outside with all the wind and sea spray, but it is beyond picturesque. I am more of a lakeside cottage guy, but if this is what the customer wants and that's the land they purchased, who am I to judge? *Please don't fuck me over Dick Dodd.* I think he has been a bit elusive, almost like he's trying to get away with something, which has made me pretty weary, but I might just be overthinking.

We finish up, and I head home to the solitude of my little cottage on the edge of the woods. When I pull in, a recognizable green four-runner is parked in front of the garage. She came. I hold back my excitement. Coming to talk to me in person could be the end, or it could just be the beginning.

Chapter Twelve

Kira

*T*his is fine; everything will be fine. Just tell him the truth.* I chastise myself while waiting in Ben's driveway. I'm not sure why I decided to see him in person. *Yes, you do, you whore.* I chuckle to myself; *I hope seeing me and seeing his reaction will soften whatever is holding me back from this relationship. Then we can make up the way we did on our first date.* The heat of that memory runs through me. *I have never felt so much at one time before. Longing, lust, warmth, joy, unease, and excitement all at once. I am falling for this guy, but I don't want to rush this, even though we already skipped all the bases and ran headlong into home plate.*

I am jolted from my thoughts by the sound of gravel under tires and look up into the rearview. Ben's black truck pulls into the driveway, right next to me. I look over at him; his eyes smile with that handsome, lopsided grin. *He's probably wondering what the fuck you're doing here.* I think loudly. I smile back and slide out of my car. Ben comes around the front of his truck to meet me. *Do I hug him or kiss him?* The decision is made for me; Ben grabs me and pulls me into his chest. I smell mountains, winter, sage, and the smell of the woods; I can only describe absolute contentment in one scent.

"Hey," he says with a gravely low voice into my hair.

"Hey, I'm sorry I just showed up," I rush out.

"Never apologize, remember. I am happy to see you." I could hear the smile in his voice even though I couldn't see his face. I pulled back and looked up into his greenish-gold eyes.

"Are you sure?" I am constantly questioning.

"Yes, do you want to come inside? I need to shower quickly, but can you hang out with Crash?" He says with a smile that melts me from the inside out. He releases me and takes my hand. Leading me to his front door and Crash. "Crash sit! Calm down, this is Kira," he croons. Crash doesn't care who I am; she busts out the door. We watch as she rips around the yard until she finds the perfect spot to do her business. He looks down at me, "She fits her name, huh?"

"She does, she's adorable!" Pups always make me excited. I look back, and Crash is coming full bore. I bend my knees, awaiting the impact. SLAM! I am sprawled out on the floor with this huge chocolate lab all over me.

"CRASH!" Ben booms, "Get off her!" He reached down, hauling her off me.

"It's okay! I was prepared, did you see me bending my knees" I say, rubbing my butt; that *is going to bruise.* I think to myself with a wince.

"As long as you're okay, I will shower and change. I stink," he says while giving himself. *I don't think you smell bad; you smell delicious.* I think to myself, watching him turn and walk away.

"I'll be here with Crash! Take your time!" I shout as he reaches the bathroom door; he turns and looks over his shoulder. With a wink, he disappears into the bathroom. I sit here on the couch watching Crash devour her dinner; all I can think about is the fact that Ben is in the bathroom naked. *I bet he looks magnificent, freshly showered, dripping with water, and with a toned body wrapped in a towel that probably barely covers his form.* I might be drooling. I shake my head, chuckling to myself, *stop, you need to talk to him about what's bothering you.* I do need to tell him about what happened.

While he is in the shower, I flashback to the day before I asked for a divorce:

I am in the living room of the old apartment in Riverside; I can feel the carpet between my toes. I am drinking, drinking so much tequila. I am swimming in hate, anguish, and disgust. I hear the door open and look up. I have the phone records in my hands. I have a positive pregnancy test, and I want none of it. He looks at me and sees… He sees everything; he moves too fast. Ripping the bottle out of my hand and chucking it across the room, glass shards are everywhere. I pull out of his grip; I can't breathe.

"Kira, there is glass everywhere," he says as I walk away from him toward the bedroom. He lunges for me and throws me to the wall; he growls in my ear. "Don't be stupid, Kira; no one will believe you anyway." He looks down, "what is that?" Pointing at the pregnancy test.

"I'm pregnant," I say dryly in a voice that feels foreign to my own.

"Well, it's not fucking mine, you are a cheating whore."
He spits at me; he is incorrect. I am not a cheating whore;
I am pregnant with his child. Though I refuse to be any
longer.

"I'm going to get an abortion tomorrow," I tell him. His
grip tightened.

"You're damn right you are," He hisses.

"And I want a divorce," I say with so much determination
I almost forget I am drunk.

"You what?" He asks, only feigning confusion.

"You heard me when you told me I should just divorce
you. That I hate you, why stay." I do not waver, "I am taking
you up on the offer now." For once, the asshole is speechless.

The next day, we went to the abortion clinic. It turns
out there was no baby in my uterus, but the ultrasound
technologist couldn't see if there was an ectopic pregnancy
(found outside the uterus, which can be life-threatening).
"What a fucking waste of time," Avery yells on the ride back
to the apartment.

"Well, not really; if it's ectopic, I could die," there is no
emotion in my voice anymore. "I'm going to the emergency
room when we get back," I exclaim to no one.

"I am not going with you." He says flat out, "I'll be packing up my shit so I can leave as soon as possible tomorrow.

"Fine by me, you can fucking take it all. Except Winston." I growl. He just looks at me like I am insane. "Do not touch a hair on his head."

I hear the shower shut off and pull myself out of the dreadful memory.

***

Ben

Kira Logan is sitting on my couch in my living room while I am naked in the shower. I resist the urge that comes over me in the shower. I can still smell her beautiful scent in my nose. Her warm body was against me; her arms were wrapped around my waist. I turn the hot water to a colder setting to bring down the man downstairs who loves every inch of Kira. I speed up my shower with the new temperature, then get out and dry off in record time.

Putting on my slippers and wrapping a towel around my waist, I open the door and head to my. I apparently catch

Kira off guard because she is staring. *Is that, is she drooling?* I think with an outward chuckle. "Take a picture. It will last longer," I say with as much sarcasm as I can muster; red crawls up her neck and brightens her beautiful face to a full pink.

"I… I was…You startled me; that was a fast shower," she shutters out, turning even more red everywhere.

"I was just pulling your leg, Kira," I chuckled and continued to the bedroom. I slipped in and shut the door with another wink, which I hope did the trick.

***

Kira

I AM FUCKED. I have shaken off the flashback, but how am I supposed to talk about important things when he looks that sexy? He was all dried off, but his hair was still damp, and God that wink. It shoots electricity down my body and causes things to happen that don't need to happen right now. *It's okay, focus; we just need to finish this so I can put it in the past.* I think while I wait. I hear movement closer to the door, the knob turns, and Ben comes out wearing a red flannel and black jeans. "Well, hello," I say, smiling like an idiot.

"Hello to you too. Now, what's on your mind? Do we need to cancel for tomorrow?" He says with a furrow to his brown. The couch sinks as he sits beside me, causing me to fall a little into him. I look up, and he looks so concerned. There is worry behind his dark eyes, watching every move I make. I clear my throat, "So you remember I was married?" I ask because who doesn't remember that catastrophe? He nods, and I continue, "Well, I am totally over him. I have been for a long time, but something recently threw me off balance."

"What happened? Did he hurt you?" the deep rumble and set of his jaw tell me that if he weren't already dead, Avery would be a dead man.

"No, no, he hasn't hurt me in a long, long time." It's probably a mistake to say that because Ben goes stiff. "I promise I'm fine. My brother Oliver called today and surprised me with some news." *STOP BEATING AROUND THE BUSH, KIRA.* "He's uh, he's dead," I mumble.

"Oh shit, I mean, I'm not mad that he's gone, but what happened?" He relaxes and focuses on how I am feeling, it seems; he grasps my hand warmly and tenderly.

"Well, he's been out in Alaska for almost six years, I think, since the divorce." I take a breath, "He went overboard during a storm. It took them almost a week to find his body washed up on the Alaskan coastline." He nods, inviting me to continue, "Well, it seems he must have died that last night of my last weird dream about him." I rush out, Ben's eyebrows furrow in confusion.

"You think he died that night?" He questions.

"Yes, maybe he was drifting in and out when I had all those dreams, and maybe that last one was it? Maybe part of me just knew he was gone, which is why it is so confusing." I look away; tears are forming. I know why I'm emotional, but I'm worried it will anger Ben.

"It makes sense to me; dreams have a way of helping us deal with things and sometimes preparing us for what could happen." He says with all seriousness. *Well, shit, he does get me,* I think to myself.

"Oh, I wasn't expecting you to get what I was trying to say. I don't love him anymore, but the dreams were extremely unsettling. I hate him, but I don't wish death on anyone. Maybe a little bit of maiming," I laugh. "It caught me off guard all the emotions that went along with the news, and

I didn't want to bring into this relationship. I spoke to my therapist and Penny, and they both agreed that the emotions are normal." I explain.

"They are normal, Kira, and it's okay." He is so kind; his words do things to me… I need to tell him more.

"There are some other things that I believe I should tell you; I want you to have some context. I won't tell you everything, but I will tell you this." I told him, waiting patiently for his response.

"Whatever you need to do, Kira," He takes a moment to breathe, "I am not going anywhere." He tells me, honestly lacking all his words.

I take a deep, steadying breath. "It is an incredibly long story, but I will tell you a story." It is only part of the story, but I will tell him the day I caught him cheating—cheating on my twentieth birthday.

It was my 20th birthday, and my friend Alana visited me from Illinois. We spent the day in Jeffersonville, Ohio, doing what girls do…shopping. We got home, and after all the travel, Alana needed a nap. I walked into the apartment and led her to the guest room. I didn't see Avery anywhere; our apartment had a fenced-in courtyard. There was access to the area behind the apartment through that courtyard. I noticed he had left his cell phone on the table as I went outside. His phone lit up with a new message; I remember feeling wary of looking at his phone, but when I glanced at the name, I noticed it wasn't a saved contact. It was, however, an Ohio number; I didn't even know Avery had any friends here in Ohio other than our neighbors.

I made the mistake of looking. Picking up the phone, I read, "Oh, Avery, when you are going to come over again, I miss you, and JD misses you." I sucked in a breath and kept reading, "JD has been talking about you non-stop since you came over last; he's not the only one who misses you." I was in utter shock. Who the fuck is this? I still remember wondering if she had a child. My husband was at another woman's place, playing with her child while I was what? At work? Sleeping? When would this have happened?

I heard an engine start, but it wasn't a truck or car. Making my way out through the courtyard, I saw him starting a fucking dirt bike. A dirt bike he did not have this morning when I left to go shopping. He looked up and smiled. The smile hit me because he had no idea that I knew or that I was shattering inside. He lied. He promised me he'd never do this to me again, but he did.

"Hey baby girl, look at this!" he says with too much excitement. I don't understand why we had a new dirt bike on my birthday.

"Oh wow, um, why did we get a dirt bike?" I asked, completely confused.

"Because I wanted one?" Like not talking to me about this purchase was no big deal. I skipped that response to that all together. I lifted his phone in the air, and his face dropped.

"Who is this? Who is JD?" I question, with my face showing no emotion.

"It was one time." That's all he said.

"That isn't what I asked Avery." I was going to kill him. This is happening all over again. First, it was the girl; 8 months ago from Maine that he "wasn't going to have sex with," but they were just friends. I forgave him; we worked on it. That was the first time he brought me flowers and the moment I stopped loving flowers from anyone.

"Kira, I promise it only happened once," he said, raising his voice. I put my finger to my lips, and tears escaped my face.

"Alana is upstairs asleep." I whisper-shout, *"We will not discuss this again until she leaves. She will kill you if she finds out, and I won't stop her."* I turned on my heel and walked into the house.

I look at Ben, "I am not proud of what happened next." I tell him, "I forgave him again." Tears slide down my face, "but I didn't forget." Ben doesn't respond right away; I do not expect him to. I just hope he will still be open to loving me back.

"Those emotions are normal; you may not have liked them, but you're human, Kira." His eyes are gentle and understanding.

"That's exactly what they said," I huff out. I'm a little frustrated that I overreacted. "Well, that was it; I was all twisted up inside worrying about what you'd think of me and what I thought of myself... I," he interrupts me and drags me into his lap.

Pressing his lips to my forehead, "It's fine, Kira. I'm not worried about what happened; I only care about how you feel and whether you're happy." He looks into my eyes as if seeing all of me. I put my arms around his neck, and he smashes his lips to mine. He puts his hands on my waist, rearranging me so I am straddling him. He moans into my mouth as he devours me, nipping my lips and exploring my mouth with his tongue. He breaks the kiss and begins to trail kisses from my ear lobe, *fuck, that is wonderful,* all the way down my neck to the collar of my shirt. I am moaning now because, my god, that feels good. I can feel the butterflies and tingles; I want him.

Chapter Thirteen

Ben

I pick her up and carry her into the bedroom, kicking the door closed. My knees reach the mattress, and I toss her onto a bed. A squeak comes from her that drives me crazy. She giggles and looks up at me, eyes hooded and dark with need. *She has no idea what she does to me. She's driving me crazy.* "Do you want me to devour you? Make you forget everything that has ever hurt you and just make you feel me?" His voice was low, filled with lust.

"Please, please just make me feel you!" She almost screamed. I had been dreaming about this since our date. Reliving everything in your mind is not the same as feeling it. Without hesitation, I climb onto the bed and gently remove her clothes. I stand back on the floor. My gaze traveling all over her devouring her with my eyes. I slowly remove my clothing; each button on my flannel unbuttoned felt like an eternity… Next, my jeans, undoing his belt, unbuttoning, and unzipping. She is almost out of breath. Her chest rises rapidly as I finish. Pulling down my pants and boxer briefs together, my cock springs out and pulses with need as she stares at it. She licks her lips and pounces.

★★★

Kira

I roll onto my knees, pushing his shoulder back to the mattress. His eyes go wide, and then, as if he knows exactly what I am doing, he relaxes back, and his eyes become hooded. I lean in and kiss him gently at first, then feverishly. Trailing kisses down his body to where his body creates a natural v; he is so beautiful. I could kiss and touch him forever. I reach his length and touch him tentatively, gently moving up and down him with my hand. I looked over at him, his eyes fixed on me with anticipation. I lean in, continuing the eye contact, and fill my mouth with his length.

As I take him deeper and deeper into my mouth, I can hear his breathing change. With each movement, his breaths become heavier. Small moans escape his lips, and his hand creeps up my arm, to my shoulder, to my neck, and finally into my hair. I relish the feeling of him on me; it's incredibly hot to have him guide me up and down with his fingers in my hair. He grasps my hair tightly and rips my mouth from his cock; I smile because I could tell he was close.

Removing his hand from my hair, he whispers, "Get up here, Kira." I move off him and up his body, climbing on top of him and leaning in for kisses. I am soaking wet sitting on his belly/pelvis. "God, you're incredible; I could do this forever," he admits, eyes ever leaving mine.

"Me too," I rasp out, so turned on I could combust right here.

"It's your turn," he says as a form of a warning when he lifts me and rolls me simultaneously so he is now above me—resting between my thighs, placing kisses along my inner thighs, driving me nuts. All I can do is lay back and relax, waiting for the immense pleasure to run throughout my body like a volcano eruption. He touches my center with his index finger, moving through my folds, "You're so wet for me, baby." Leaning in and kissing me where his hands just were.

He begins to devour me, over and over, sending pleasure through my body. I can't even believe this is real; a person can bring me this much pleasure, and he is enjoying it. He loves to eat me out as if I am a three-course five-star meal. I cannot stand it; my legs are shaking, and sheets are bunched in my fists, so I don't grab him with my fingernails. He continues, and I keep climbing closer and closer to release; he slides a finger inside me. I gasp, relishing it as he slides another deep. Curling around and rubbing me from the inside causes my body to shake uncontrollably. My walls squeeze his fingers, pulsing around him over and over till. I am cresting, falling, cumming all over his hand and in his mouth. Over and over, I pulsate around him. He continues to extend my orgasm, *holy shit, that's amazing.*

He stops, resting his head on my inner thigh, waiting for my orgasm to wain and finally finish. "You are amazing," He whispers, "absolutely the sexiest woman I have ever had the pleasure to hold." He says with lust, or is that love? I can't tell the emotion behind his hooded, dark eyes. He slowly raises and climbs over me, "Are you ready for me, baby?" He asks with the sexiest rumble that I can feel throughout my entire body.

"Yes, please, I can't wait to make you cum." I say, a little embarrassed but not caring because I feel incredible. He holds my face in his hands and kisses me; he kisses me with all the emotion and feeling I saw in his eyes moments before. He lets go of my face, and I feel the loss of his heat immediately; he leans over the bed to his nightstand to get the condom. I help him rip it open and roll it onto his length. Once that task is complete, he settles himself between my thighs, nudging my entrance. I gasp, "Please, baby," I whimper.

"As you wish," He whispers into my mouth as he simultaneously pushes deep inside me, taking my breath away and kissing the air out of me at the same time. Either way, I can't breathe. I am so complete, so full of him, of emotions. *Do you dare say it, not in your head but out loud?* Those three words are on the tip of my tongue; I am falling so hard for this incredible, sweet, attentive, and caring man.

***

Ben

Jesus Christ, she tastes so sweet and so good. I could lay here torturing her for hours, but I need this. I think I missed her so much: her smell, her smile, and her body. I continue to thrust into her, filling her to my hilt. We change positions multiple times, and everyone feels even more fucking amazing than the last. *I could do this for the rest of my life, this perfect girl.* Shaking those thoughts away, I think we've only seen each other for a week. But it feels like she has been mine forever. Like everything was leading to this moment. If she could read my mind, she would laugh at me, but damn, I am falling for her ocean-blue eyes. I am drowning in them as I watch her take me inside her, unable to hold still with pleasure. She pets me, drags her nails down my back to my ass. Squeezing, she pulls me harder, faster into her. I am so close, and she knows it; she can see it or hear it, how she knows.

"Cum for me, Ben, please." She gasps, begging. I oblige her, I move faster and a little harder and cum so hard there are sparks behind my eyelids. Filling her, I hold onto her, refusing to let go because this is everything.

"I could do that forever," I kiss her neck. She stills, almost like she is thinking about what I said.

"I could too, Ben. This is the best I have ever felt. You make me feel like the only girl in the world. As no one else matters, it's just me and my pleasure," she says with what looks like pain in her eyes and longing.

"You've never been so thoroughly fucked that you felt like this before?" I ask because this woman is incredible, and it would be an absolute shame she hadn't been worshipped before.

"No," she says sheepishly, "I've never orgasmed by a man before; I have faked it or used my vibrator when I'm alone." "You're the only man who has ever made me cum, period." She says with such finality.

"Well, I am glad I can give you this, and it doesn't end here. I will make you feel worshipped for as long as you have me." I say because I would do this forever, but I don't want to scare her. Her smile shines.

We get up and make our way into the bathroom. Showering together, I feel like I could take her one more time if she didn't have to get home to have dinner with her parents and take care of Winston. I wash her body and her hair, holding her and loving her like she so deserves.

Once dressed, I walk her to her car and kiss her, "Thank you for telling me what was going on. I know that sometimes it can be hard, especially since we're still learning each other." I say, "But I am always here when you need me." I kiss her forehead again.

"Thank you, Ben. I was so worried I'd ruin whatever we had, and I just couldn't. I care about you, and I could be with you even with all the baggage I have." she says with a wobbly voice. I take her in my arms and hold her in place. *Kiss her so she knows that no matter what, I'm here, always.* I lean down, dropping a gentle kiss on her adorable soft frown. Her lips curl into a smile beneath my lips as I hold her cheeks in my hands and deepen the kiss. *I could do this until the end of time; I* have never had that thought about a girl until her. Kira Logan has completely stolen my heart. She gets into her car and slowly heads down the drive toward the roadway; in a few minutes, after staring at her retreating car form in the shadows of dusk, I turn and head into the house.

154

Chapter Fourteen

Kira

Looking in my rearview as I head towards my parent's house, I wish I could stay here. Fall asleep in his arms and let our life begin. But it's too soon. We've only been together a few weeks. But here I am, wanting forever; I am the girl who rushes everything and falls hard into relationships, but I don't want to do that here. I want whatever this is with Ben to last. *Should I take a step back?* I think as I continue, listening to "Left and Right" by Charlie Puth. Singing the chorus at the top of my lungs, I drive down every back road, every left and right turn it took to get home.

I walk in the front door, my mom is still moving around the kitchen. Dad is already in bed, and it's almost 8 p.m., so that can only mean one thing. Mom wants to talk to me about

Ben and what happened to Avery. "Hey, Mom," I say as I walk into the kitchen.

She looks over her shoulder, "Hey Kira, how was your day?"

"It was okay. There were a lot of emotions, but I am okay now, I think," I say in a hushed tone. I don't want to wake Dad if I don't have to.

"I heard. Oliver called me and told me about Avery." She says resigned, "He said you didn't sound okay. I thought you'd be happy, not hurt. What's going on?" She lifts her brow in a questioning gesture; I know all too well.

I take a deep breath, "It isn't that I was upset about the news, per se, but I was startled." I take her hand, "Can we sit on the couch? I want to catch you up on some things happening to me, including my emotions." We walk hand in hand into the living room and ease onto the couch; I lean in close because this is my mom. She will love me no matter what I tell her, but she doesn't know half of the trauma I endured so many years ago. I told her about the dreams that happened over a week, which were confusing and upsetting. I tell her about the last dream, that he had me in his grasp, that I got away, but I turned back. I went back into that torture apartment that haunted my dreams for years after the divorce. I told her about what he said, *"I cannot change what I did, but I… I am sorry."* A look of anguish passed over my mother's face, "With all that being said, finding out that Avery most likely died during those last dreams scared me, Mom." I say, voice trembling.

"Oh, Kira… Avery made his decisions, and you did nothing wrong." She whispers into my hair, "he hurt you; he ran away instead of facing the truth." "Did we all wish he'd drink himself to death or hope he'd drive off a cliff? Yes! But he let you live your life instead." She says, believing every word, "he left the area, so if you came home, he didn't have to face you. That also means you did not have to face him either." She gave me a small smile, "It's going to be okay, my girl. You feel so much; I know you get that from your dad, but I feel a lot, too. Sometimes I don't know how to express it like you do." Resigned in that confession.

"I know, Mom, I don't hold it against you, but sometimes I wish I didn't feel so much. That I could just be happy that my abusive ex-husband could die, and I couldn't care less." I confess with tears leaking down my cheeks. "I was so scared

I canceled my date with Ben, which was stupid." She looks at me, then a bit confused.

"Why did you cancel? He had nothing to do with Avery, right?" She asks.

"No. But he is a person I am falling for, and all those emotions and the ones that live in my heart. I didn't want them to get mixed up and have a trauma response that involved Ben by default." I say, "I met with Penny in town for coffee today and talked to Julie; they both had the same opinion." I take a deep breath and let it out slowly. "I'm an empath, and I am hurting because someone I knew so intimately died."

"So, what did you do from there? Did you talk to Ben?" She still looks confused.

"Yes, I went in person to talk to him." The red that crawls up my neck is unmistakable, and she will know. But she does not say anything about it.

"Well, I am glad you could talk to him and tell him what was happening. Being able to communicate your feelings is huge in a relationship. You will avoid a lot of misunderstandings and fights." Giving me a knowing look and my intimate knowledge of my failed relationships, she knows me sometimes better than I know myself. "I haven't seen you smile like this in a long time, Kira. Don't let this one get away." She whispers into my hair, kisses me on my head, and pads off to her bedroom with my dad.

***

Ben

Laying here, I can still smell Kira in my bed. Her beautiful floral scent envelops me. I can close my eyes and see deep into those ocean-blue eyes. It almost feels like I can drown in them.

It might be time to talk to my mother. Kennedy Alexander is not only my mom but also my best friend. That sounds lame, but it has been me, her, and my brother for a long time. I have no interest in being in my father's life, so she gets it all. All my news, the good, the bad, the ugly, the scary, and the sad. Since I am obviously falling in love with his girl, I have to tell her. I have been smiling and increasingly upbeat; she must suspect something. A buzzing comes from my nightstand; it's like she is reading my mind. Looking at the screen, I see a picture of Mom and me at my high school graduation, "Hey, Mom, what's up?" I ask because God knows already.

"Benjamin, are you seeing someone?" She sounds clipped.

"Oh yeah, Mom, I was going to..." She interrupts me.

"Who? Gossip around town is that you are smiling more, and I haven't heard from you as much." There is hurt in her voice, "That usually means you've met someone and either don't want me to know, or you've just been to be enamored?" She has a giggle in her voice; she can't stay serious about anything, but she can try.

"Her name is Kira Logan," I admit with no restraint, "She is pretty incredible, Mom."

"Oh, I have heard of her; didn't she leave the state for a while?" I open my mouth to reply. "She's got great parents. I think they have worked at the hospital as long as you've been alive." She laughs, "When am I going to meet her?"

"Soon, I want to have a few more dates, and then I promise you'll meet her. She is something different." There is a choke in my voice. "She's beautiful, strong, intelligent, and she just wants to be loved."

"Oh well, I can't wait to meet her; I'm sure I'll love her too." My mother been waiting for me to settle down. Probably because she wants grandkids, but I hadn't found the right girl. "Well, I just wanted to call and get the gossip from your lips and not the town grapevine. I will let you get to sleep; I love you, Ben." She makes a kiss sound on the phone.

"I love you, Mom. Good night," I say. She hangs up, and I am lost in my thoughts about Kira again. Do I text her now or wait until the morning? I hate that relationship rules that have changed so much over the years. Why can't I call the girl I'm crazy for without it being a big issue?

Ben 21:00 [Hey Kira, I hope you made it home okay. I just wanted to tell you that I can't wait to see you tomorrow night for dinner.]

Kira 21:01 [Oh, Ben, I did. I'm sorry. I should have texted; my mum was waiting for me, and I wanted to tell her about everything that was going on. I'm headed off to sleep now, though. Good night <3]

Hmm, I can't tell if she is upset with me or just tired. I won't overthink it. I will see her tomorrow and think I'll ask more questions than while writing my message back.

Ben 21:05 [Oh good. I don't think there's a need to be sorry, remember? It sounds excellent to me. I am beat :) From the long night, sweet dreams, Kira.

With that, I fall asleep to the smell and thoughts of Kira Logan. *I am royally fucked, but in such a good way.* I think *I don't know if my heart will ever recover if things don't work out.* With those last few thoughts, I drift off into sleep.

Chapter Fifteen

One Month Later...

Kira

It has been such a wonderful month; I have gotten more hours at work, and my relationship with my parents has been great. Most importantly, I have been staying with Ben a few nights a week, and we spend the weekends glued together. We go for long drives and walk in the woods, and he is determined to teach me how to drive his tractor without destroying the transmission. I almost get it, but it's an old machine, and I prefer automatics. Our communication has improved since our talk about the past and what happened to me. We can discuss important things that bother us and what we want for our futures. Everything is just so easy, except… The Dodds, Ben's customers, are going to be the death of him. They keep changing things and have gotten tighter on their purse strings. It makes me wary of the working relationship with them, because I have a horrible feeling about that couple.

I have been working a bit more and building up my savings account. My life has not been entirely together for the last ten years, but I am a girl who can save her money. I don't live outside my means; I pay every bill on time, and anything left goes into a savings account. I have enough for a down payment on a house, but I am not ready yet. I have only been home for a few months, and things with Ben are amazing; secretly, I want him to ask me to move in so that we can see where our lives take us. I love waking up in his arms; our coffee dates in the early morning before he goes to work. I return to his bed while he's gone and sleep a bit more before heading home to get ready for work. We have introduced Crash and Winston. I was worried because Win isn't really into having other dogs around. He is a very jealous boy. But they get along great!

I get Win ready to go, and we hop in my four-runner. It's a Thursday morning in July, and the humidity is hitting, making it a bit suffocating. Mind you, Maine does not get all that warm, but the humidity and I do not get along. I also hate sweating, and I would rather freeze. It may sound crazy, but I don't mind the winter. Warm house, coffee, warm blankets, snow, Maine winters are picturesque. Summer is beautiful but crowded; no one comes flocking here when it's snowy and cold, at least not to my neck of the woods.

I pull into my parent's house. I hope I can get in and out without getting too distracted. I get Win all fed and settled on the couch while I shower and get dressed. I only work till 3:30 today, so I'll have time to come home, grab Win, and go back to spend the weekend with Ben. *Hmm, Ben, I miss him already.* I was just with him, but can't get enough of him. *CHIME* I look in my hand and speak of the handsome devil!

Ben 07:30 [Hey Babe, I hope you slept well after I left. What would you like to do for dinner tonight? I can grab something on my way home unless you want to stop?]

Oh! I have been craving tacos, so I texted back.

Kira 07:32 [Well, hello handsome, I was thinking tacos tonight? I am off early, so I'll grab stuff on my way home. I'll grab Win and be over after. Also, please do not get in that shower without me]

Ben 07:34 [Yes, please! Tacos sound great, and I'll wait for you to get home to get clean. I will also wash you and then make you dirty all over again]

Oh my, he is so naughty. I could do this forever, playing and being sexy. I think as I say:

Kira 07:36 [Oh yes please, do all those things. When we're done, I'll need to take two showers.

Ben 07:37 [Alright! I have to go before I get in my truck hold you hostage for the day. ;) Have a great day, I'll see you tonight.]

Kira 07:39 [Fine. See you tonight. <3]

With that, I pocket my phone and make my way to the hospital with thoughts of that beautiful man on top of me and loving me all night long. *God, I am in so much trouble. I am so far gone; I am in love with Benjamin, which is terrifying.*

It is okay because he isn't anyone from your past. He is the present.

*

Ben

Pulling into the driveway, I see Kira isn't here yet. I can clean up the house and get Crash's energy out before Winston gets there and is too tired to deal with her dose of crazy. I do a quick clean around the house, get the shower ready, and hang up the towels when I hear a gravel crunch in the direction of the garage. Crash starts barking like the loony tune she is. Stepping outside, I see her climbing down from her four-runner; my heart is beating hard in my chest, and my desire for her is instant. I am immediately met with an urge to take her right here in front of the house. "Hey babe," I shouted from the front. I am greeted with that beautiful smile as she turns to see us on the front porch. Winston comes bounding toward Crash as they chase each other; Kira comes up the steps and gives me a long and longing kiss.

She pulls back, eyes meeting mine. The desire, ever present in her ocean blue eyes, "Hey." She says in a low sexual tone; with a squeal, I pick her up. I wrap her beautiful legs around my waist and whistle for the dogs to follow. We are all in the house; I kiss her and take her to the bathroom. I cannot get enough of this woman. She rakes her hands through my hair, rubbing herself against my rock-hard cock. With the door locked behind us, I set her down and strip her naked as she attempts to unbutton my pants. Once she's completely naked, I take in her perky breasts, nipples peeking with desire. She reaches towards me and finishes what she started; my cock jumps out of my pants as she drags them down my body. Her eyes are dark, a smirk grazing her face as she looks up at me.

The water is running, and we jump in. The kissing, petting, licking, and tasting do not stop. With a quick rinse, we are back in my bedroom. I have her right where I want her, Kira's legs spread, waiting for me. My mouth is watering as I take in the sight of her; she is already glistening in response to our shower. I bend down, slowly tasting her; I am unable to be gentle; I have been thinking about her pussy all day. Her sweet taste, the sounds she makes when she cums, and the heat of her as she clings to me. I work her slowly, pressing a finger deep inside her as she moans and pulls on my hair. That pleasure that's almost as painful as she tugs on my scalp. She is writhing beneath my mouth; I hold her ass in my other hand. "I'm so close, Ben, OH god." She whines, begging me to finish her off. I lick and suck her clit hard, finishing her off while she moans, almost screaming my name. Her entire body convulses between my mouth and hands; I lick and lick, trying to draw out her orgasm.

I pull my mouth and hands away; she whines again, trying to pull me back to her. I climb up her, kissing her deeply, letting her taste herself on me. It is so hot to watch her lose her mind. As I make my way down, my cock grazes her entrance, and she moans into my mouth as I retreat down her. When the aftershocks finally stopped, I lay beside her arms behind my head, waiting.

"You're turn," she looks at me with a wicked grin. She is climbing down my body, kissing a trail down my front, along my happy trail. Till she reaches my groin, she cups my balls in her hand firmly. Taking me into her mouth, she fit my cock deep inside her mouth. Looking up at me, she drives me nuts because Kira looks stunning down there with my dick in her mouth. She takes me in and out, and in and out, gently licking my tip as she pulls back. Going down for the final time, tears spring to the corners of her eyes. "Are you okay, baby?" I ask, genuinely concerned she hurt herself.

"No, Ben, I'm fine. It's just the gag reflex causing the tears." She wipes them away and takes me in again. *My god!* I scream in my head... Reaching down to pull her up to me, I growl, "Please, baby, get up here. I need you to sit on me right now."

Her eyes twinkle as she lets me lift her on top of myself, "Yes, please." She says with that beautiful mouth. Bringing it down to mine, I take her lip between my teeth, nipping and biting, kissing her senselessly. Kira gets onto her knees and eases herself onto me. I am in heaven. I love this girl, but it hasn't been that long. *Don't scare her away; she might be a runner.* I think to myself, *show her you love her.* That's what I do: taking her on top of me, I fill her around and make her mine from behind. I start placing a trail of kisses from her beautiful ass to her gorgeous neck, listening to the intoxicating sounds coming from her...

***

171

Kira

I wake up wrapped in Ben's arms, warm and safe. It's Saturday, so we have nothing to do except this. I can't believe how connected I feel to him. *Don't overthink it, Kira; you love him and have no idea if he loves you, too. He has to love me.* His arm stirs beneath my cheek, and I feel his hand trace up the side of my body. I kiss his hand once it gets to my face. He wraps his rough, hard-working hands over my face, and I could die right here. The feel of his hands on me makes fireworks explode in my heart. I roll in his arms and look into his hazel-green eyes. *Don't say it, don't say it.*

"Good morning, beautiful," he says with the most devastating, sleepy smile.

"Good morning, handsome; how'd you sleep?" I ask, knowing that we both slept like the dead.

"Like a rock, I could sleep next to you forever," he whispers.

"Me too," a shy smile places on my face at the admission. "I want to tell you something, but I am scared," I say, taking my thumbnail into my mouth and worrying about it.

"I do, too, and it's okay. I'm not going anywhere," he rumbles. He takes my hand away from my mouth and holds it in his, looking into my eyes as if he can read my mind.

"You do? Are you sure?" I questioned, a line appearing between my brows.

"Yes, Kira, I think I know what you're talking about. Will it scare you away to say it out loud? Or are you done running?" He knows that I get scared easily and don't allow anyone this close to my heart. I nod as my admission. He turns entirely towards me, pulling me close, holding my face in his hands, eyes never leaving mine. He traces my lower lip with his thumb. "I love this mouth, this face, this body, this mind. I'm not scared to say it, Kira, I love you." He confidently admits the twinkle in his eyes that I love so much, showing me his entire soul. He isn't lying; he does love me.

"Oh, Ben, I love you so much." Tears appear in the corners of my eyes. I haven't said that to anyone since Avery. I have never let anyone this close in 8 years." The admission stings my eyes because I have walled off my heart for so long. It felt like an elephant got up and finally was no longer sitting on my chest.

"Good" was all he could say before he crushed a kiss on my lips, kissing me almost to pain to the most perfect pain. He continues to make sweet, hot, lust-filled love to me. Whispering, he loves me into my ears every chance he gets. *He does love me, and I love him*; I fully admit to myself for the first time in so very long.

Chapter Sixteen

Ben

We spent Saturday in bed. If we weren't there, we were on the deck watching the dogs play and fight over their toys. *Today is a big step. We talked about it a little bit last night, but I would say I'm a little nervous. "Are you nervous?" I ask, knowing full well she is,* but maybe talking about it will help.

"Um, yes." She giggles with unease.

"What are you nervous about?" With a knowing grin, I ask.

"It's your mom. You know the whole meeting the parent's thing freaks me out. She raised you, and if I had a boy, I'd be a nut. I don't know how I'd handle meeting his girlfriend that he LOVES." She says with so much sarcasm.

"She's going to love you; she's been hoping I'll settle down and have grandbabies for her," I said with a smile, "My brother and I have both struggled taking that final step," I admit with a shrug off my shoulders.

"Well, I'm not scared. I'm just a little nervous. I've been married before and divorced, and some parents don't like those things in a perspective for their baby boy." She looks at me through her lashes, nervous. What she doesn't know, I've talked to my mom about her for the last week. I've been telling her stories and making sure there aren't any surprises. My mom is ecstatic to meet Kira, and so am I, if I'm honest.

"She will love you, don't worry. Now let's go eat brunch with her, and you can see for yourself." I grab her hand and drag her to the truck. We're leaving the dogs here to hang out while we go and meet my mother. "Don't be nervous. You look beautiful. You are beautiful, inside and out."

"Thank you, sweetheart; I'm sure it will be fine too." She smiles at me for real now with that twinkle in her eyes, "Do you know why?"

"Why?" Genuinely curious.

"Because we love each other, you can see it from a mile away. With that, who could be mad about a girl loving her son." The confidence in her tone now, she believes it, and so does it.

I put my hand on her leg, squeezing it, "I love you, Kira," I assure her because it's true. *I have loved her since she was almost squished on Main Street. Then she kissed my cheek and walked away.*

***

Kira

I take a few measured breaths. *This is fine, it's okay, I'm fine.* I repeat to myself as Ben comes around the truck to help me down. My eyes meet his, and he gives that cocky side smile that does so many things to my lady parts. I squeeze my legs together to alleviate the ache. Walking to the front door, he kisses my head, whispering, "It's going to be fine; I love you." I nod and take another deep breath for good measure.

The front door opens, and a woman who is probably an inch taller than me with lighter, caramel brown hair and eyes almost the same shade as mine smiles back at me. She looks so much like Ben; they have the same facial structure and features. It makes me wonder what exactly his father looks like because he is definitely her son.

She takes Ben into a big hug, squishing him tight. She lets him go and turns to me, immediately enveloping me in a hug. She says, "Oh, Kira, I am so happy to meet you; Ben has told me so much about you." She winks.

Breathe, Kira, she likes you; breathe. I smile but can't really feel it because I'm so nervous, "It's so nice to meet you, Mrs. Alexander."

"No, no, call me Kennedy," she insists. Pulling back from me and leading us into the beautiful tan cape-cod-style home. She lives a little over a mile from my parent's house; I'd be lying if I didn't think that was such a crazy coincidence. I grew up a few streets over from Benjamin, and we never crossed paths; Kennedy lives in a different house now but is still just down the road. We all sat down for brunch.

Kennedy knew some things about me. Mostly from the gossip train, but we spend a good portion of brunch getting to know each other. My anxiety about the brunch drifts away.

His mom is fantastic. She makes me feel so welcome and at ease. I could spend all day here, but Ben has big plans for us.

Alright, Mom. I'm taking Kira away for the day, and it's a bit of a drive, so we should head out," he explained.

His mom gives a knowing look and a little bit of an evil gleam in her eye. "Oh, that's okay; I gave her my number so we can continue talking without you," his mom responded with a wicked laugh.

Great," the eye roll that came out of Ben was epic.

"Hey, be nice! She is great, and I will be talking to her without you," I say with a toothy grin.

"Sounds good to me, cutie," Kennedy says as she scoops me up in a hug. I love it; I am a hugger and a touch person. I need human contact, or I won't survive, and the feeling that Ben's mom likes me makes me so happy. *You are worthy of love*, I tell myself. It took a long time to get here, but I am here and worthy of love from others.

***

Ben

That was terrifying. I have only brought a couple of girls around, and they haven't passed my mom's test. From the outcome of the brunch, Kira passed with flying colors. My mom isn't hard to please, but her opinion does matter to me; the fact that she loves Kira means the world. I can't get the smiles and joy that were surrounding the table at brunch out of my head. We left about an hour ago and are heading up the coast to Bar Harbor. I haven't been in a long time, and neither has Kira. We plan to drive up to Cadillac Mountain and walk around the downtown area until we find the spot for a late lunch, then drive back.

I didn't consider the amount of driving, but it's nice; we are able to talk. It's the first time I haven't had the music on in a long time.

I have never been comfortable with absolute silence, but with Kira, it doesn't feel oppressive. She regales me with stories of her time in the military, and I tell her about all the trouble I've gotten into over the years. We also discuss how crazy it is we grew up right down the road from each other, but our paths never crossed until ten years after high school. She asked if I had noticed her in high school, and of course, I had. She was beautiful, bubbly, and a social butterfly. The beauty hasn't changed, but she isn't as social as she once was, and I'm not as quiet as I used to be.

"Did you notice me?" I ask, skeptical of the outcome.

She gives me a knowing look. "I knew who you were, and I could pick you out of a crowd, but I had the biggest crush on Conrad," she says quietly, almost with a pained expression.

"You what?" I am speechless; she had the hots for my older brother.

"Yeah… it was a long time ago; I was working at the grocery store, and it was a crush. No big deal." She shrugs. Her head goes to her chest.

Honestly, I don't really care, but seeing her squirm is hilarious. "So, you still have the hots for him?" I ask, knowing the answer.

"WHAT! NO!" She yells loudly and pushes my shoulder.

"Hey, I'm driving here!" I could not contain my laughter as she pouted in the corner of the truck seat. "Kira… I'm kidding!" I laugh but sober quickly as I notice the tears pooling in her eyes.

"Yeah, yeah, sure you are." She whispers.

"I'm sorry, Kira. I was really kidding. Just trying to get a rise out of you." I say gently and put my hand on her knee.

"I know, I guess it's an immediate insecure response. When I was with Avery, I was accused of so many things that I didn't do, and I don't know why, but it brought a little of those feelings back." Her voice sounded so small. I pulled the truck over on the side of Route 3 and reached across the seat. I unbuckled her and dragged her small frame into my lap. Taking her face into my hands, our eyes are glued together, nose to nose.

"I am not Avery; I did not mean to bring you back there." I tell her clearly, "I would never do anything to make you feel that way; I will never accuse you of things I know you would never do. I was messing around, and I am sorry," I say; she leans into the inch between us, and I capture her lips in mine. I held her so tightly that there were a few loose tears. *Such an ass,* I chastise myself.

"It's okay, Ben; I'm sorry I got so emotional." She whispered into my mouth, "I'm not usually like this."

"Honey, don't ever be sorry about your reaction; we all have them." I remind her.

"Okay, well, I'm okay now." She exclaimed and moved off my lap, buckling back in and smirking me. I put the truck in the drive, and we continued our trip down east.

***

Kira

He isn't Avery; get out of your head and enjoy yourself, I tell myself repeatedly. We make our way up Cadillac Mountain in Bar Harbor; I remember coming here as a child. It was a foggy day, and you could not see much from the top but it still seemed awesome. Today, the sun is shining, and I can see the harbor, which is full of sailboats, lobster boats, and even yachts. The wind blows my hair around my head, whipping and twisting; Ben leans down and drops his hat on my head. Surprisingly, it fits me well, and my hair is no longer whipping in my face. I step up onto my tip toes and kiss his soft, rosy cheek. The sun may be out, but it's chilly on the coast. Ben wraps his arm around me, and I snuggle into the warmth he radiates.

"Don't those small islands that look like huge turtle shells popping out of the ocean?" I look up at him, seeing if I'm insane for the thought.

"You know, I see it! At this level, there are four that look almost the same, and that could be giant sea turtle islands." His low chuckle does things to my stomach. "You're so freaking adorable, I love you." Leaning down, he kisses my forehead with the gentlest touch.

"I'm not nuts then?" I raise an eyebrow questioningly.

"Absolutely! We're all just a little crazy." I elbow him in the gut, "Ooof." He grabbed his side.

"Don't be rude," I say, "I'm sorry I didn't mean to do that so hard."

"Ugh... It's fine; you're just on kiss probation." He exclaimed with a cocky smile. I roll my eyes and get back in the truck. We have to make it back down the mountain and grab lunch before we make the almost three-hour drive back to Hamlin.

We decide to go to Geddy's. This fantastic restaurant with a beautiful harbor view. They sell t-shirts here, and I am a sucker for novelty t-shirts. I smile up at Ben, "Can I get a T-shirt?"

"Get whatever you want, beautiful; it'll look great on my floor with the rest of your clothes." He whispers into my hair.

"Oh, really, Benjamin." I am getting warm all over because that sounded like a promise, not a threat.

"Oh, yes, Kira. It has been a long drive here and back, so when we get home, you're mine." The heat in his eyes is unmistakable. God, if we weren't in public, I'd let him take me right here on the restaurant table. A tall brunette steps up to the table. My face feels like fire when she asks, "What can I get you guys?"

"I'll have the Shrimp and Scallop scampi and a Coke Zero." He recites his order like a champ while I'm trying to get my brain to work properly.

"Great, and you?" She also asks. The name, Gabby, is displayed on her chest.

I decide to make it easy on myself. "Gabby, I'll get the fish and chips and a water," I reply with all the confidence in the world. *Breathe, Kira, he's just messing with you,* I think to myself, trying to get my arousal under control. Gabby steps away to enter the order and get our drinks.

"You're in so much trouble," Ben growls.

My eyes go wide, and my face reddens again, "What, why?" *He's messing with you, Kira.*

"You're naughty, and I can't wait to get you home." His eyes were dark with lust, and he growled at me.

***

Kira

"Ben! Stop it!" I cannot contain my laughter as Ben throws me over his shoulder, and a fireman carries me into the house.

"You've been naughty, Kira; you know exactly what the punishment is," he growls while nipping the soft, exposed flesh of my waist next to his delicious mouth.

"I didn't do anything. You're a crazy man!" I cannot stop laughing. We let Crash and Win out, and he carries me to the bedroom. The door shuts behind him with a click, and he tosses me onto the bed. A squeak escapes me as he drops me.

"Now, are you ready?" He asks with a glint of mischief in his eyes.

I have no idea what he has planned, but I don't care, "Yes, please." I pant.

"You're in trouble for being the sexiest woman I have ever laid eyes on," he says, "You're being punished for stealing my heart." He climbs over me and crushes his mouth to mine. His kiss is so firm, and he's taking my breath away.

With my mouth full of his, I say, "Oh no, I am so bad!" he continues to kiss me as he starts stripping his clothes off, piece by piece. First, his shoes and socks. Slowly, he undoes his belt, and off go his pants. His briefs are creating a tent of his hard cock; now, he releases my lips to rip his shirt off and start undressing me. I wore a sun dress, sandals, and underwear, but I have no bra today. He reaches up my dress and slowly slides my soaked silk panties off my body. He drags the hem of my dress up my body painfully slowly, and he devours my body with his eyes. This process may be fast, but time slows as he looks at me. He was making me feel like the most delicious thing he's ever seen.

"Lay back, baby," he rumbles out as he spread my legs with his rough, hot hands. "Let me taste you, I have been thinking about your pussy all day." I do exactly what he says; I want to let all the pleasure he gives me flow through me.

I can't control the moan as he licks circles and nibbles on my swollen clit. I was drenched; I was already soaking wet when he threw me down on the bed. He places one finger inside me, playing me like an instrument of lust. He puts in another finger and finds that magical spot that undoes me. I am panting and so, so close. All at once, he pulls back; I whoosh out a breath, wanting to scream.

"I was so close, Ben," I cried out.

"You are naughty, remember? You need to be punished first." He threatened. Hot, I am so fucking hot right now; he stands from the bed. His briefs still create a tent, but there is a spot of wetness at the tip. He moves around the bed and grabs a box. Inside the new box, there is a beautiful teal vibrator, and *oh god, he's going to torture me.* "Lay down on your back, keep your hands over your head." He instructs me.

I do as he says, legs open with my arms above my head. The bed shifts as he eases his body onto the bed. He turns the vibrator on a high setting with a mischievous smile. He presses the magic device to my clit, and my god, "Ben, don't stop" *I can't believe it,* "I'm, I'm so close," I rasp out. Immediately, he pulls away, and the loss of friction is awful. "WHY!"

With a knowing look, he says, "Are you going to be a good girl and cum for me?"

"Yes, please, make me cum." I am begging now; the loss of contact is driving me insane. He places the vibrator back on my clit and starts to finger fuck me. In and out, in and out, there are stars behind my eyes as I fly headfirst over the cliff of my orgasm. He continues to lick and circle my entrance to lengthen my orgasm but also to taste me. He gets up onto his knees and leans over me, giving me a wet kiss with my taste on his lips. He lays on top of me.

Placing a hand on my ass, he rolls so I land on top of him. I continue to kiss him and rub myself against him; I'm so incredibly close to another orgasm. He lifts my hips and drags his briefs off his body, grabbing both my legs placed on either side of his muscular pelvis and gliding me on top of him. Usually, our sex is hot and languid, back and forth, with lots of pushing and pulling of orgasms and moans. This feels different, though; he gave me orgasm after orgasm, and now his eyes filled with heat and another emotion. *Is that love?* I think, I know he told me he loves me, but if that's what love looks like in his eyes, then my god, I could die right here. "Are you okay, baby? Is this okay? I want to take you slow, agonizingly slow." He breathes lust, love, and pleasure written all over that handsome face.

In answer, I leaned down, grasping both sides of his bearded face, and kissed him hard and wet. Reaching up, I place my hands on the headboard and begin to ride him, slow and deep. My breast hangs heavy about him as he goes between licking, sucking, and nibbling my pebbled nipples. My nipples are so hard they could cut glass with the arousal running through me. The slow friction of sliding over his long hard cock makes me get close again. "Cum again for me, sweetheart; I want to watch you cum all over me." He growls into my breasts.

"I'm so close, Ben, oh god…So… close!" I scream, "BEN, JESUS CHRIST." I have never come on top of someone before, with my walls clenching around his hard cock and my wetness causing us to be slick and drenched.

"You're so wet for me, baby," he rolls me onto my back, "I want to taste you." I don't argue, he descends and moans into my wet throbbing pussy. He relishes my taste, cleaning me up and preparing me for his continued exploration of my body. He sits back on his heels and lifts my hips to meet his dripping tip. *I've never had sex without a condom, but I have an IUD, and my god, I don't even care at this point.* I think as my mind swirls with desire. He plunges into me, ready for his orgasm. Pumping into me like I am the only way he will survive, in and out, deep to his hilt. I can feel him throughout my body, deep in every corner. My heart is so full, and so is my body. "I love you, Kira; oh, I'm going to cum," he rasps, "I'll pull out."

I grab his hip and hold him inside me, "I have an IUD, your fine baby." I say with so much confidence I don't even know who I am right now. "I love you too; fill me up." With a wicked smirk, eyes lidded, he does just that. With his silent orgasm racking through his body, pulsating over me, I take in his beautiful body, his face, his mouth, and the incredibly sexy hands he has holding me still with. *I have never felt a love like this.* I speak to myself while I relish everything I am feeling in this perfect moment with Benjamin Barnett.

Chapter Seventeen

Two weeks later...

Ben

Everything is hitting the fan currently; we are getting close to having the interior of the Dodd's place completed, but they have decided to order a kitchen package without informing me that it is more than twice the allotted budget. It's arriving tomorrow, and I have to adjust my framing to accommodate the taller, more intricate cabinets.

We are behind. I had to let a guy go for his other job, and I had to fire another because frankly he was incompetent. Richard, who truly embodies his nickname "Dick", says that they want to be in for Thanksgiving and since we are heading into the middle of the summer, and that might not happen. I have one guy helping me, but he's not a finish carpenter. I hope this does not end up fucking me in the end. I hear a chime from my pocket and I pull my phone out of my pocket:

Kira 11:05 [What do you want for dinner tonight?]

Ben 11:07 [Oh honey, anything as long as I get my favorite dessert :)]

Mmmm, Kira Logan for dessert, I think as I wait for a reply.

Kira 11:08 [You're naughty! I can make whatever. It's going to be warm. Do you want to do burgers on the grill?]

Ben 11:10 [That works for me, honey; I'd love that. I'll call you when I'm on my way home.]

Kira 11:11 [See you then, honey bun. I love you <3]

Ben 11:13 [I love you, Kira <3]

I can't believe she loves me; I can't believe I have fallen so hard for this girl. I think to myself as I get back to work. *Do not fuck this up; ask her to move in with you.* I don't want to wake up every day without her anymore.

****

Kira

I don't have a ton to do today. I took Winston on a walk at Dodge Point this morning, and we got to see a seal basking on the rocks, and he got to chase some squirrels through the trees. It's times like that when I am so grateful to be back in my hometown. My state, the world I grew up in. The only place I have ever been where I feel at peace and safe. *You are safe; you aren't alone.* I tell myself as we sit on the porch together; Win rests his head in my lap. I would genuinely be lost without this sweet, gentle boy.

I have therapy in about five minutes today with Julie. I have so much to tell her. It has been a while since our last session, and I have been going less frequently since being home. I'm just excited to tell her about what is going on in my life, and I have questions I want to ask her before I talk to

Ben. *Ringing* I look down. My therapist is a bit early for our call, but I'm not mad.

"Good afternoon, Kira. How are things going?" Julie asks in her calm, therapeutic voice.

"After everything that happened the last time we talked with Avery and Benjamin, I am doing well," I say without hesitation. *I am okay.* "I wanted to ask if you thought it was too soon in my relationship with Ben…" I hesitate now, "Maybe we should move in together?"

"Oh! Well, that depends on how Ben is feeling. You guys have been seeing each other for a few months now; you don't have anything tying you to staying with your parents. If you guys are happy and can set the effective boundaries we always discuss, I think that should work fine." She says, "but it isn't a decision I can make for you. You need to talk to Ben and find out what he is looking for in this relationship."

"He told me he loves me," I whisper.

"Kira, that's wonderful. Do you love him too?" she asks with a bit of excitement in her tone. I always have bad news when we talk, or I am in a dark place, so this must be a nice change of pace from our normal sessions.

"I do; I think I fell in love with him on our first date. We went to his house and walked onto his property, and there was a willow tree next to a secluded pond. In the tree, there was a plank tree swing. He helped me onto it, pushed me, and just watched me swing and enjoy myself. I felt so free in that moment, so safe and well… Loved that I fell headlong into love with him." I admit to my therapist of 8 years.

"Well, Kira, I think that is incredible, and if you say he loves you, I don't see why moving in together wouldn't be the next natural stage. I hope you communicate what you need and know how to get what you need in the relationship. I have given you enough of the tools you need to deal with any issues that arise. But Kira, I think it will be wonderful." Julie telling me her opinion means more to me in some ways than hearing my parents. They had been there for me over the last few years but didn't know everything about that relationship. They never will. Some things are too much to relive. "Do you have any concerns? How are you doing mentally with the death of Avery and the nightmares?" She asks; she knows me so well.

"I have been doing well; I shouldn't have kept what was going on from Ben or my family; I just felt insane and didn't want to worry anyone. But, I am doing a lot better now." I explained.

"Well, I am glad you opened up to the people you love, but I am also glad you called me when that moment was too much for you. You know what you need, and that shows great progress and healing. I am proud of all of the progress you've made over these last few years." Julie affirmed.

"Thank you, I appreciate you saying that," I tell her honestly because it really does mean a lot to know that all the mental work I have done since the divorce wasn't for nothing.

"That's the end of this session. Do you want to make another appointment, or do you want to do a monthly check-in next month?" She asks. She has never asked me to just do check-ins before, but it makes sense. We haven't had a session in a while, and I should probably have something set up that isn't an emergency session for my own sake.

"Yes, let us chat again in a month or two. What do you recommend?" I asked Julie because I was curious about how she wanted to schedule these new "check-in" appointments.

"Let us try one month for now, and if things are still settling in and you feel comfortable with that, then we will talk again in one month. I hope you have a wonderful month; keep your head up and remember the tools you have spent so long learning." She speaks to me with such kindness, and it is no wonder I keep coming back. I need someone unbiased who knows the line between wanting to comfort me and knowing when to let me know that what I am saying is not healthy or helpful. I tend to have unhelpful thoughts that work against my mental health.

"Perfect, thank you, Julie." We hang up, and I think about everything I have gone through and found out about myself. *You are not the problem; you are not the reason he cheated; you are who you are.* I was lost for a long time but since I have learned to love myself. Love who I am for who I am. I'm not just the wife who got cheated on, the divorced girl in her twenties, or the grouchy Airmen who would get yelled at for attitude. *I am Kira, I am beautiful, intelligent, hardworking, and I won't take shit from anyone ever again.*

Four o'clock rolls around, and I pick up the burger meat, buns, cheese, ketchup, frozen French fries, and brownies for dessert. Apparently, bachelors have no edible food kept in their houses. I have also grabbed Coke Zero because it's the best; he knows it's my favorite and doesn't mind drinking it instead of anything else. I get here before him, so I let Win and Crash outside and ran them to get out their unending energy. I'm alone in his house, so I take the time to glance around. Pictures of himself and his mom, pictures of Crash throughout the years, and all the bowls he has made. He makes the most beautiful things with his lathe and hands.

I daydream about his craftsmanship when I hear the dogs outside bark in unison. I look out the front windows, and there he is. The craftsman himself looked so incredibly handsome. Mussed hair from a long day on the coast, most likely on a roof. His warmly tanned arms, sexy hands, and that handsome smirk. He makes eye contact with me, but the pull is unreal. I feel like an invisible golden thread connects us. A thread that, when we're apart, almost aches, but when he's near, it seems to pull me, drag me into his arms, and wrap around us, leaving us in a world of our own making. I have dreamt of a love like this; I'm not sure I ever believed I would find his. In his arms, I am warm, safe, and loved.

***

Ben

Pulling into my driveway, I see her four-runner and the dogs losing their minds outside. While I'm walking up the driveway, I see her. She's standing in the window in the yellow sundress she wore on our first date. My eyes meet hers, and it's as if she can read my mind. She disappears from the window and is immediately in my arms. I smell her beautiful floral scent, her golden hair shining in the July sunshine, warm and perfect. She looks up at me, "Hey, handsome," she says against my lips in a wet and needy kiss.

I pull back, "Well *adorable snores. Just do it,* my mind insists as I continue to kiss her. We make our way into the house and close the bedroom door behind us with a click.

***

Kira

As I lay here breathless in the arms of the man I love, like truly love, all I can think is… *Am I enough? Would he want a future with me forever? Am I temporary…*

"What's going on in that pretty little head of yours?" He asks me with genuine curiosity in his eyes.

"Oh, nothing, just overthinking, my usual," I let out a self-deprecating laugh.

"What are you overthinking?" he asks genuinely with concern, lacing his tone.

"It will most likely scare you away with all my over-thinking ways," I whisper. *He is not a part of your past but your present. You talked to Julie, and she agrees this is a good step…* I think, at war with my mind and my mouth.

"You won't scare me away; I love you, and to tell you the truth, I have been doing some thinking myself." He looks sheepish.

"You have… is it good or bad?" I ask. *My heart is racing like a beat, and I don't know if it will explode or stop altogether.*

"I wanted to know if you wanted to move in with me so I don't have to wake up without you anymore. We could work on the addition we have talked about and make this little house ours?" He stops talking and holds my face in both of his hands, doing show slowly makes my eyes well with tears, "I want to be with you, and I don't want to sleep without you anymore." "I want to know you'll be home when I get here or at least know we will be together at the end of a long day." He says almost breathlessly, eyes never leaving mine.

Tears are now running around his thumbs, "I was worried you thought we were moving too fast; it hasn't been that long, and we've already said we love each other. Maybe all of this was in my head, that this was a dream, and the other shoe would drop any moment." I rasp, "I would love to live with you; I would love to come home to be with you after a long day, make dinner together, and have our pups become forever best friends." I lean in with a wet face and kiss him soundly.

"Perfect, now let's get something to eat. I am starving," Ben exclaimed, *but to tell you the truth, I was famished!*

Chapter Eighteen

Beginning of September...

Ben

We are getting close to the deadline of the Dodd project; we've had a few issues... One of my guys sawed off the end of this finger, which was an unforeseen circumstance. The orders for windows and doors were delayed. Even though it has been two years since the pandemic cursed the world with death and the inability to perform everyday life, we continue to deal with delays; enough that the end of September deadline I thought we could meet is quickly approaching, and we aren't finished. We will most likely not be able to put the finishing touches on until at least October, making it a 13-month project. One month overdue. Now here we are, one and a half months till I can get this project buttoned up, and I have received the down payment for the final push on the house, but that was mid-August. I need to pay the plumbers and electricians before I can finish this project and get my final labor bill.

I drafted an email with the project's final cost, which was about $50,000 over the original budget due to the changes the Dodds made to the project. I need to pay for the lumber yard as well. The email states that we are ready for the second to last payment of the contract. In August, I sent a final invoice outline; I needed a deposit of almost 1/3 of the final payment cost to get things paid. The final bill is about $100,000; in August, Dick Dodd gave me $30,000. Last night, I sent an invoice for second installment, and I'm still waiting to hear back. I called Dick this morning, with no response. I texted and resent the email. Again, no response before we packed up for the day and left the job site.

Thankfully, Kira was home. When I pulled into the driveway, it was about 11 a.m. She was sitting on the porch watching the dogs play. She gives me a beautiful grin, which I felt to my toes. She has been living with me full-time for a couple of months now, and it has been heaven. We mapped out a plan for the addition to give ourselves more room in my small house.

"You're home early." She shouts to me.

"Yeah, Dodd didn't pay me, and he's not answering." I was as restrained as possible without yelling or expressing my true feelings about the situation.

"Well, that's bullshit. Maybe he's in a meeting and didn't get the email? Or calls?" She says because she is ever the optimist. I am looking for the best in everyone and hoping for the best.

"I hope so. Want to go for a ride? Or go to the beach; there are only a few more nice days before the cold rolls in for the fall?" I ask; I want to be with her. We could be anywhere and be doing anything. It does not matter to me.

"Yes, of course; let me put the dogs in the house, and we can go." Her eyes twinkle, and she touches my arm, which always makes my heart swell. She has a way of making everything feel okay. I got here, I was fuming, and she was just here; she knew not to push or ask too many questions.

Kira is genuinely one of a kind but in my mind… *I hope to God that Dick Dodd doesn't take this away from me too. I cannot let my anger for this man to ruin my relationship.*

***

Kira

We jump into my four-runner and head away from the coast; with everything going on, the ocean doesn't need to see us today. We make our way inland toward the lake; I know of a secluded spot I used to go to when I wanted to be alone. We are on the outskirts of Hamlin, on an old back road. There still aren't any signs of trespassing, and I have no idea who owns this little sanctuary, but we will deal with that if we get into trouble. Ben looks at me with confusion; he doesn't know where we are, but why would he?

"Where are we going?" He asks tentatively, "This isn't some serial killer place where you secretly dispose of bodies?" He's kidding, but I can feel a touch of anxiety radiating off of him.

"You listen to way too many true crime podcasts." I laugh because he is insane. "This is where I used to go when things were tough. I have no idea who owns it, but it isn't marked with no trespassing, and it never has." I say a bit sheepishly cause no doubt we are trespassing without a sign.

"Alright, honey, lead the way." He says, trusting me with everything, all of himself.

"Let's go," I say. He takes my hand, and we walk the short distance from the car to the edge of the lake. There is a very old but sturdy bench and a rope swing. When Ben finally sees that the rope swing is attached, his eyes go wide.

"A willow," he whispers to no one in particular. He looks at me with a knowing look.

"I told you they were my favorite. This was the tree I fell in love with. This is the bench that listened to all my teenage problems. This rope swing threw me into the water when I needed to reset. This tree was my haven when I had no one and didn't know what to do with my anxiety." I tell him, "Come sit with me."

He does, but he does not let go of my hand as we make our way around the tall grass and ease onto the bench. "Thank you." That was all he'd say. We sit for an indeterminate amount of time, allowing the world to buzz around us. The sun was shining so high in the sky when we got here, and now it is making its way west. It has not crested the tops of the trees, but it will soon.

"Are you okay?" I ask; it was long enough that I hoped I would not ruin the sanctity of this place with questions.

He looks over at me, "I guess. I am incredibly frustrated, but this has helped so much." He says, leaning down to kiss my lips. He wraps his arm around my shoulder; I lean into his warmth. "It is just so disappointing for someone to hire you because of the quality of your work, but in the end, they will not pay me for that work. They would rather not pay at all. I will never understand that... I can do nothing to make him pay; no cop will force someone to pay what they're supposed to even though it's technically stealing." He growls, "If I would tear out 70,000 dollars' worth of work out of it and call it even. That prick will not even call me back." He says with a sigh.

"I'm so sorry, Ben, but maybe we can fight it?" I ask. Ideas have been brewing in my mind all afternoon. I think I can figure out a day to make this better, but he has to continue to trust me.

"How? I am relying on that money; we could add-on to the house." He fumes, so angry but trying to hold it all in…

"I have an idea, but you need bear with me." I give him a cautious, almost nervous smile.

"Kira… what are you thinking?" I am genuinely curious about what I might have up my sleeve.

"Marshall Damien." I don't have to say anything else; he knows exactly who I am talking about.

"He is one of them; he is from Massachusetts! Why would he help us? He is probably related to that asshole." He was vibrating with frustration.

"No, he isn't. He has lived here for a long time. I may have been gone, but I still know he has been here since before I left. He also went to law school and is a contract lawyer; he can fix this. I know he has helped other builders in the area." I say, "I investigated him when I got a bad feeling about Dick Dodd. I hoped it wouldn't turn out this way, but I had a bad feeling and thought we should have a plan." I admit, I worried he would be even more angry.

His expression softens, "You're amazing, Kira. I can't believe you researched him. If you he could help, I am willing to talk to him." He says, worry lacing his voice. "I don't want this to come between us, Kira; I can't lose you, too." His eyebrows were almost touching, and the anguish in his eyes was palpable.

"Ben, I have been through hell, and this is not that. If I can survive being emotionally tortured and hurt, then I can be in your corner. I will fight this battle beside you." I interjected, "I will not let you sink; the whole time." That is a promise I can keep. We got back in the car and made our way back; As we drove back, he made the call because, right now, it was his business. We set up an appointment with Marshall Damien, and now we wait.

Part Two

Chapter Nineteen

January 1st…

Ben

Marshall R. Damien, Contract Law, or Marsh for short. He is the lawyer for the builders in our area. An out-of-towner who grew up in Massachusetts, although according to the grapevine, he doesn't claim Massachusetts as his home. He moved to our small town of Hamlin 15 years ago, five years before Kira left, but she heard about him. Marsh and I weren't friends per se, but he was a damn good lawyer, and with what was happening, we needed this cleared up.

After Dick Dodd did not respond to any of my emails or calls, and since it was no longer the summer season, he had not returned to the home in a while. I decided to talk to Marsh and get this all taken care of. Marsh put a mechanics lien on the house, which put some pressure on Dick and the bank. He did not realize I had the money to have a lawyer, but the jokes on him. After the lien, Dick responded. He claimed we did not finish the house on time and the cost was much higher than the initial quote. He also claimed, and I quote, "We were unable to have precious memories with family in the house this year, and you cannot put a price on that." *Fucking tool is you ask me.*

Over the last few months, Marsh has been working on our case. There were some issues with how my contract was written, and I needed to put in change orders for some things. Even with all the problems with our case, state law states that "Obligation of good faith" should be enough for what we are dealing with. I completed the changes to the building as requested by the customer, which cost more than what had initially been quoted in the contract. We collected witnesses from the lumberyards and subcontractors who knew about changes and were present for conversations.

Marsh thinks we could win this, but I have my reservations. Kira has been my champion, getting paperwork together and ensuring the tasks at the house are running accordingly while I do other work, so I don't lose my employees.

We are conducting a meeting at the house tonight; it's Kira, Marshall, and myself. We have our first meeting with the mediator tomorrow and want to be on the same page. Marshall will do most, if not all, the talking so I don't get angry, and Kira will play the supportive adorable girlfriend who will fuck you up if you cross her. "No tire slitting tomorrow, Kira," I say pointedly.

"What, it was only a joke," she rolls her eyes. "I would never do something illegal… Well, not in broad daylight or the courthouse parking lot." He evil gleam in her eye; I could take her right now, but fucking Marsh is here.

"Please don't do anything to get yourselves in more trouble," Marsh says between bouts of laughter. "I'm a contract lawyer, not a criminal defense lawyer. I mean, I could swing it, but no promises." That got all of us laughing; I am surprised at how much I like Marsh. He was a massive help with everything, and everyone was right. He does have our back even though he is not a local by birth. *So, it turns out neither is Kira. Her parents moved here when she was a baby, but I do not hold it against her. It makes a lot of sense, though.* I think to myself while watching Marsh and Kira go back and forth about what is and is not illegal retaliation.

"Has he called you more since we started this?" Marsh asks me, concern written on his face.

"No, just those few times I told you about; I told him he could talk to my lawyer, and I hung up. Since then, he hasn't tried." I shrug.

"Good, he has no business attempting to make contact; he is in the wrong, not you," Marsh explained for the hundredth time. "I'm going to head out and get some rest. It will be a long day tomorrow. You folks should get some sleep, too, so you do not look so cranky." With that, he stepped out into the frigid January cold.

"Well, we should go to bed too, huh? Wait for tomorrow to come?" I speak with sarcasm, lacing every word.

"I have a better idea; let's have sex and pretend we won, then wake up tomorrow and win again!" Kira whisper-yelled as she jumped onto my lap.

"That I can do.!" I pick her up, throw her over my shoulder, and carry her into our bedroom. Once there, I lay her down gently and begin stripping her naked, kissing and loving every inch of the woman who consumes my every thought and keeps me from completely losing my mind. She smells like flowers and tastes like candy; I am intoxicated. She is my drug; I make my way down her neck, kissing and licking. With a tender nibble, I bite each of her perked perfect nipples, which pulls the most delicious moan from her throat. Continuing down, I lick her tattoo that runs down the side of her body, licking every curve of the cursive letters that make up the Tolkien quote. She isn't ticklish, but this somehow causes a ripple of awareness that brings goosebumps to her flesh all over her beautiful body.

Once I make it to the top of her lacy panties, I pull them down so achingly slowly that I think I might die of excitement. Looking up into those beautiful blue eyes of hers that I love, they have now turned pitch black. Desire takes over; her legs are quivering, and her hands cannot stay still. She has moved them into my hair, directing me where she needs me most. I begin kissing her inner thigh, slowly getting closer and closer to her soaking-wet pussy. Desire coats her inner thighs. I dive in headfirst, literally. I lick, suck, bite and work her into a complete and utter tizzy. I push one finger inside her opening, in and out over and over. I add another finger, knowing it is exactly what she needs, pushing and pulling at the same time I pull her orgasm out. Dragging it slowly and intensely, she always puts her hands over her beautiful face as she orgasms. She screams my name into her hands as she comes all over my lips.

Once she has come down, the pulses of pleasure slowly rise above her. I kiss her beautiful mouth with her taste on my lips. I love her mouth; the wetter her kisses are, the more turned on I get. I am already about to rip through my work pants.

"Get inside me, please," She begs into my neck. Her hands are all over me, scratching and pulling at the fabric of my shirt, my pants, and my hair. I oblige her and stand, undressing as slowly as humanly possible in front of her. The amount of frustration that grows on her face is everything. The heat and lust coming off her is astounding. Once I am free of my clothes, she spreads her legs as wide as she can, showing me all of herself. My confident, beautiful, and perfect match, and she is all mine. I prowl over her and push inside her. *Fuck* is all I can think, *she is perfect. This, I could do this for fucking ever.* With everything that is happening, I need her to know how much I love her.

I make sweet love to her at first, but she doesn't want me to be slow and sweet. "How do you want it, baby?" I ask, knowing the answer.

"You know what I want," Sex coating all of her words.

"Say it," I demand.

"Fuck me, Ben, bend me over on this bed and fill me." She panted, "Fill me over and over till you explode inside me. I want to feel you drip down my legs."

"Fuck honey, you're going to make me cum with those dirty words alone." I am not lying she is so fucking sexy; I could blow my load right here. She wiggles out from under me and gets on all fours. Looking over her shoulder at me, wagging her butt at me like the sex goddess she knows she is. "You asked for it," I whisper as I sink inside her to my hilt. The moan that exploded from her, I am so achingly close, but it doesn't matter. She wants me and the immense pleasure I bring her.

With that, I give her everything she asks for; pounding in and out of her until her body tightens and quivers. She screams as she topples over into her orgasm. I explode inside her shaking and pulsing with my release. Pulling out of her, I stalk to the bathroom. I clean her up with the dampened cloth and tuck her into the covers. She is sated; she could fall asleep here and now, but I can't let her do that. I pull her in close to my chest and poke at her, attempting to keep her awake a little bit longer. "I love you, Kira," I whisper into her hair when I place a kiss on her head.

"Hmmm, I love you, Ben." She says quietly, sleep coming fast.

"Thank you for everything. I would not be here without you. I wouldn't be this okay without your support." I admit. She opens one eye, squinting at me.

"You wouldn't be this sexually satisfied either." She quips and closes her beautiful blue eyes again.

"True, but I am serious, Kira. You have made my life 1000% better by being here with me." That kind of admission is hard for me. I do not share often, but it is the easiest when Kira is sleepy. She does not push me for more; she just takes my words to sleep with her.

"You make my life 3,000% better, Ben. Now go to sleep." With that, she puts her head down on my chest, and her once-rhythmic breath slows to a calmer and quieter rhythm that I can barely hear but can feel.

I whisper, "Goodnight, Kira; I am going to marry you one day." The confession is easy because it is true.

Chapter Twenty

Kira

He thought I was sleepy, but in fact, I was not. I was just so incredibly comfortable; the confession warmed my entire soul. Ben was not a man who did things he did not want to do; Ben was a man who would only do something if that were indeed what he wanted. That he admitted wanting to marry me, well asleep me, says a lot. *DO NOT OVERTHINK OR FREAK OUT, KIRA*; I chastise myself. I know that he will not ask me any time soon because of everything going on, but to know that he genuinely loves me. To know that this love is not one-sided. With that, I fall into a deep, undreaming sleep.

The following day, a text comes through from my cousin Paysen Scott. She lives across the pond, and we have only recently made contact. Our mums are half-sisters, and we never spent time together as children. We have slowly built a cousin-cousin relationship that I adore. I wish we could have been close as children but having her in my life now means everything. She is supposed to visit America soon, and I cannot wait to tell you the truth. I cannot wait to introduce her to Ben. It seems I will be getting my wish, "Hello love, it *looks like I'll be in America in the fall sometime! I am hoping to swing in and see you either before or after.! I hope all is well. Speak to you soon xx.*" I do a little happy dance; Paysen *is coming to see me!* I respond with so much excitement and roll out of bed.

We get ready like we do every day. The mediation is at 10 a.m., so we run to the job site to get the guys on track for the day with tasks on this new job that they cannot screw up. Ben's crew is re-siding a house in the harbor. Today, they are stripping the cedar shake singles and prepping for new siding. So, fingers crossed that today will be less stressful. We have not seen Dick Dodd or his wife at all since this started, But who comes to Maine in the winter when you also live in the Northeast.

"Here goes nothing," Ben says with trepidation in his tone.

"I got you! You know that, and I did bring my box cutter, so their tires are toast if this goes poorly." I say with a sheepish and a bit evil grin. He stops our forward motion and crushes a kiss to my lips. We both need it, and I relish every second we have. Footsteps approaches us but doesn't halt our embrace. The cough that let us know that we genuinely were not alone. We both swivel out glances toward our friend Marsh. "Hey, Marsh, just giving him some of my good luck."

"Yeah, I can see that, and so can the rest of the town." Marshall was not impressed, with a touch of haughty to his stance.

"Don't make me hate you again," Ben shot back at his lawyer. Who is saving us today?

"Stop it, both of you; there is nothing wrong with PDA. Let's get in there and show the Mass-holes how we do things here in Hamlin. Not you though, Marsh, you are not a Mass-hole, well, not all the way." With a wide grin, I took Ben's hand and walked into the courthouse. No sign of the Dodd's being here, only an older well-dressed man with a reddened face, bulbous nose, and beaty eyes. *Yuck.* The only word I could think of when I saw that man sitting at the table.

"Where are the Dodd's," Marshall asks.

"They won't be joining us for this mediation, I am Stan Swallow." He reached his hand toward Marshall, and I had to stifle a laugh because Swallow as a last name is hilarious.

"Interesting. This is mediation, where our clients work out the issue, and we are here to assist them in any way possible," Marshall responded, ever the gentleman with such ice lining every word.

"Well, it is January, and travel to another state is not always safe" A tall chocolate brown-haired woman with red-rimmed glasses says. She sits down at the head of the table and observes the conversation stoically.

Marsh stops our conversation and gives his attention to woman.

"Hello, everyone. My name is Linda Haines. I will be the mediator for this case." She said smoothly, with no malice or discontent. She, indeed, was the definition of neutral.

"Hello Linda, I am Marshall Damien, counsel for Benjamin Barnett. We also have Kira Logan, Benjamin's girlfriend.

"It's nice to meet you," she says. You must be Counselor Swallow," she asks.

He cleared his throat, "Yes, ma'am." He reaches out and shakes her hand, "Stan Swallow, I am here on behalf of the Dodds; with the roads and their long drive, I will be here as their representing them in this matter."

"Great, now I have looked over everything you all have brought. What exactly are we looking to have done today?" she asks, even though if she had all the information, she already knew the answer.

Marshall turns to her, "My client is a well-known quality home builder here in Hamlin, and we are looking to have him paid for work he completed on the Dodds house. He did not receive the last two payments from Mr. Dodd. The work has stopped, and a lien has been filed on his house until we receive the second payment. Once we have received that payment, Ben will finish with the work and we will ask for a signed contract that Ben will be paid in full at the end of the project. He says succinctly.

"Well, that isn't what the Dodds would like to happen," the gross-looking man bellows. "Mr. Barnett here has increased the price without any change orders or explanation of cost."

"That is incorrect," Marshall says icily and sternly. Mr. Barnett has provided pricing updates monthly, and the reports were forwarded at the time of the first third of the deposit. If Mr. Dodd had a price issue, he should not have paid the first deposit and had a conversation with Mr. Barnett."

"He tried; Mr. Dodd said Mr. Barnett was unreachable and would not talk to him about the price. Also, the timeline has extended far past the completion date, and you cannot put a price on a person's time." Mr. Swallow says with a smirk,

"Well, Mr. Dodd is mistaken; we have no records of phone calls, emails, missed calls, or emails. There was no communication that the price was an issue, and the house is 90% complete. Mr. Barnett deserves to be paid for the work he completed." Marsh stated plainly.

"Mr. Damien, my clients appreciate the work done, but it isn't the price they agreed to, and Mr. Barnett does not have change order records." Mr. Swallow grumbles. God, he was *sweating a lot.*

"Yes, and I have about 5 or 6 witnesses who were present at the times of the meeting where Mr. Dodd asked for more, asked for changes, and bought a larger kitchen package without consulting Mr. Barnett." Finally, what Marshall had said was final.

"Oh… Well, word of mouth does not make a contract." He swallowed, "Without a written change order, how would Mr. Dodd be able to agree to the new price?"

"Easy, if he wanted something and asked the builder for it, the builder would, in turn, build it. It seems Mr. Dodd did not have the sense to ask how much these extras would cost or even that they would be more than the original working price, which is his issue. Not Mr. Barnett's." Again, Marsh had an icy comeback. Mr. Swallow may literally swallow his tongue or have a coronary.

"I need to confer with my client for more details." He replied, sweating through his shirt.

"This is why we prefer to have all parties present, Mr. Swallow." Mrs. Haines looks a bit angry now.

"Lastly, we would like to inform Mr. Dodd that if he does not comply with our request, we will be suing him for the costs owed for the project, loss of wages, damages, and fraud."

"Fraud!" Mr. Swallow shouted, "How on earth did you land on fraud for this lawsuit?"

"Well, Mr. Swallow. We believe that your client is a predator. Preying on a small business, he doesn't believe he has the funds to fight back. So, he picked Mr. Barnett and his business. Playing him, adding things on, not asking questions until the end. When he plays the victim and pretends to be taken to the cleaners by the awful contractor who only cares about money." Marshall says smoothly, "What Mr. Dodd did not expect was that this community stands behind the little guy. We support our small business owners and have all watched this project happen. We watched Mr. Barnett and his crew work hard to create a beautiful product. The fact that Mr. Dodd dared not pay is beyond me."

"I… I need to speak with the Dodds before anything can decided on or resolved." He sputters.

"You should inform them that I will be coming for them if they decline this generous offer. I will take them to court, and they will never want to live in this beautiful town again." Oh, Marshall was intimidating, Mr. Swallow stood.

"I will speak with them, Mrs. Haines, and have an answer by Monday morning." Mr. Swallow exits the room abruptly, and I let out a long breath. Looking over at Ben, I realize he was silent the entire time. He did not so much as flinch when the door slammed.

Chapter Twenty-One

Monday...

Ben

Marshall fucking Damien crushed it in mediation. Today is the deadline. At noon, we will know if the Dodds want to go to court for more than they expected or if they want to give us what is owed and walk away. If they want us to finish the build, we will sign another contract, but I will never do work for that son of a bitch again. Kira was right to feel uneasy about the situation, and I wish I had taken the correct steps to cover my ass. *Never again*, I think, *will I leave holes in my paperwork that could allow someone to take advantage of us like this again.* I can't force everyone to pay, but I can work on my contracts to further break the payments and alleviate the lack of funds. The work will stop at the first sign of lack of payment, and hopefully, we will find only good customers.

Kira is all curled up in my arms as I lay here waiting for the sun to continue its progress into the sky. It has been a tense, stressful weekend. We went to my favorite spot by the pond multiple times and made love under the willow tree. She's truly a sight to see when she's unwound under the branches of the willow. The long branches swaying in the sea breeze, the rosy tone of her cheeks, the warmth of her skin as she pressed against me. I hope I never have to say goodbye to her, never have to live without her; I have never truly loved someone not like this.

She is stirring in my arms now. " Good morning, beautiful," I whisper into her hair. She looks up at me with a sleepy expression.

"What time is it?" her groggy voice tells me she isn't going to be happy about it.

"5 a.m." I cringe at the look she gives me, knowing that she is not a morning person.

"Really… Why…" She dives her head under the sheets to prevent the sun from shining in as it continues to make its accent in the sky. "It's too early; I don't want to be awake."

"I know, baby; let's get some coffee and watch the sunrise?" I ask her, knowing she will be a grumpy girl until she gets that half coffee, half cream, and sweetener in her system.

"Fine, but not until I have coffee in my hand!" She whisper-shouts, "I cannot be responsible for my actions until then." I slide out of her grasp and amble into the kitchen, letting the dogs into the yard. I make our coffee and leave it on the coffee table. If she wants it, she's got to get out of bed.

✦✦✦

Kira

It is 11:30 a.m., and we have not heard anything; Ben hasn't said a word since around 10 a.m. I believe he is expecting the worst; a lawsuit will be expensive, but we hope the Dodds will want to finish their house and not be ostracized from the community. *I can see the headlines in the Hamlin Times,*

"Out of State Couple Stiffs Local Builder" or *"The Hamlin Community Stands with Local Builder Against Out-of-Stater."* However, I will not let this get in the way of Ben and me; I will have his back and fight for him. Dick Dodd is lucky I have not seen him in town or at the mediation.

I took the day off today to be here with Ben, but part of me thinks I should have gone to work. I can feel the anger and anxiety radiating off him; he is the deal-in-silence type of guy. He will talk when he is ready; he needs to sleep and think about things before making any decisions.

This makes sense and sounds reasonable, but I am not always the most sensible person. I deal with things head-on; I cannot let things sit. I must find the underlying cause of my feelings because it will consume me entirely if I don't. Sitting here I let my mind wander; *I think about so much in this last half hour waiting for the news. Ben quietly sat next to me on the bench under my Willow tree on the outskirts of town.* I think about the past because that is where my mind goes; that is where all of my anxiety, trust issues, panic, and life changed.

Many people ask me the question, why women do not just leave? The truth is we want to. When I was with Avery, I wanted to get away. The fixer in me did not know how to fix it; I desperately wanted to change whatever was happening that was causing our lives not to work. He kept me from having friends and talking to my family, and he would say soft, kind words after every incident. After he cheated, he came home with flowers and promises. Truthfully, it seemed that, at the time, those things fixed it. I did not have a therapist, and no one would believe me anyway if I talked about it. I know that sounds cliché, but when you are with someone charming and outstanding in public but an absolute nightmare at home, who would believe you?

I remember vividly the last day we were together, the day I made him leave. *It was the last straw; he went to chuck the expensive camera he bought me for my birthday. He was aiming it for my glass China cabinet; I made to grab the camera before it went into the air, but when I did... My two fingernails caught on the skin of his chest; minor scratches appeared on his skin. The first thing he said was, "I can call the cops and prove you've abused me, you psycho bitch." I had never defended myself in my life, but these two scratches pushed me over the edge. I saw red; I said something I never thought would leave my mouth, let alone my mind.*

"You do that; I will throw my face against the door frame and tell them what you did to me. Avery, who do you think they will believe? WHO?!" Avery blanched at that moment because he knew he had pushed me too far. He backed up and said, *"Fine, keep the fucking camera. I don't want it anyway."*

So, I did. I kept my camera, and now I use it every day. Along with my phone, I use my camera to capture images of life, happiness, and love because I never want to be in the nightmare that was my life eight years ago. I never want to feel trapped, alone, or unable to leave. When I think about everything that has happened in my life the good, the bad, the terrible- it is hard not to wallow. Not to wonder *what the fuck Universe*, because really, how can so many awful things happen to one person.

I do not know how I conquered the emotions and panic that have plagued my life over the last ten years. All the anger and self-loathing, the hate that has filled my heart for so long, has finally been wiped clean. The man beside me on this bench patched and sewn back together all the holes in my heart. We are under one of my favorite trees in the world. The second lives on our property, but we are here… Together.

I look up at the handsome man sitting next to me. The worry and anxiety mar his beautiful face. His eyes, once a lovely mix of green and gold, are dark green with anger—greener than I have ever seen them. The forehead that usually is relaxed and at ease now is creased with worry, brows furrowed. We wait and wait, the two of us on this bench. *CHIME* We both look down at the phone in his palm, Marsh.

Marshall: [THEY TOOK THE DEAL! They will be paying you what you're owed. They also want you to finish the last few things. They have signed a contract stating they will make the last payment upon completion. I wrote into the agreement that if they fail to pay, we will be suing for everything we threatened in mediation.]

Marshall: [Thank you for trusting me with this, Ben. I will call tonight with more information, but until then, YOU WON!]

The breath that came out of Ben was incredible. I thought I was going to vomit when I heard the phone chime, but I kept it in. I look over at Ben. Tears crest the edges of his vision, "We did it," was all he said before he grab my face and kisses me—all the worry, panic, and love that he had built up inside him over the last few months. All of it just washed off him; in

a wave, he was my Ben again—my Ben.

Chapter Twenty-Two

Three months later...

Ben

We are loading up the last of the job trailer. I could not afford to pay Muck and Chad, so it is just Kira and me loading up. We finished Dodd's place finally, but we refused to start work till we received the middle payment. After that delay of two weeks, we finally got back to the site. I finished everything and cleaned up. There was some tile work to do, and I finished chaulking the windows and door frames. Kira is a trooper; when she was not working at the hospital, she was here working late nights to make sure that we got this shit taken care of and got away from these assholes.

Marshall made sure to include in the contract that the Dodds were not allowed on the property while we were working. Before the threat of lawsuits, one of the significant issues we had during the building process was that Mr. and Mrs. Dodd were slowly moving in. They brought in furniture and put things away when we weren't finished working yet. Not only is this a hazard to myself and my guys, but if we damaged the furniture during the process, who knows what could have happened? Although the furniture wasn't an issue for the final stages of work, it felt like they were already moving in before the house was completed. This really bothered me and Kira.

Kira has big plans tonight; we are taking a mini vacation. We're staying in a bed and breakfast somewhere in Northern Maine. Now that it's April, the snow is starting to melt there. We are also nearing our first anniversary. Kira does not know this, but I got all the plans from Ollie for where we are going and did some research. We are staying at the Chamberlain Hill Inn in Moosehead Lake. General Joshua Chamberlain fought for the Union Army during the Civil War; he was from Maine. The hotel was once a large estate that housed his family after the war. It has almost five stars on

Google, and it is gorgeous. The rooms have beautiful views of Moosehead Lake, oversized soaking tubs, and fireplaces in the bedrooms. It is well deserved for both of us, but I hope we will see some wildlife at this time of year. Kira is a bird girl; she will stop listening to a word I am saying to hear whatever bird is singing outside the window. It is an irritating quality, but it is also pretty spectacular when the smile shines on her face when she hears it.

***

Kira

We are on our way! *I am surprising Ben with a trip to Moosehead Lake. I have never been, and I cannot wait.* I have been saving quite a bit of money; Ben's mortgage is super low, so our bills only really include our utilities and phones. Ben has business expenses, but I have been able to save up. Ben has been bugging me all day about the details of our day and where we are headed. *I am a vault!* I had Ollie help me plan it because we would need someone to check on the dogs or, better yet, stay with them. Ollie offered, and I am so grateful.

"Babe… Where are we going? It is taking forever!" He whines for the hundredth time.

"Ben, it is the same distance to Bar Harbor. We did it there and back in one day! We are staying a weekend here. Go to sleep, and I will wake you up when we get there." I say while my patience is running thin. *You are a terrible liar, and he probably already knows where we're going*, I chastise myself.

"I can't just go to sleep; then you'll be lonely." He exclaimed, "We can't have that! What if you fall asleep?"

"I will not fall asleep; three hours is nothing. You know I've driven 15 hours straight before with my mom as a co-pilot." I shivered; that was the worst trip ever. "This is easy. Pick a crime show to listen to, and we can figure out who the murderers are together." We listen to "Dateline" a lot when we go for long rides; it is super disturbing but interesting at the same time. Some of the outcomes are expected, but some people get away with murder.

"Fine, what would you like to hear? Girlfriend accused of killing boyfriend or random town in Nebraska where an elderly couple was killed in their home?" he asks in the most monotone voice I've ever heard. I looked over at him, wondering what the hell he was doing.

"Uhm, that sounded terrifying. Maybe I don't want to listen to those," I say, genuinely unsettled.

"I'm kidding, ha-ha, let's do the elderly couple in Nebraska." He announces as he pushes play on YouTube.

***

Ben

Kira is a terrible liar; she is easy to read and fluster. I have been bugging her all morning, pretending I have no idea where we are going. The pink in her cheeks when she gets flustered or embarrassed is adorable. We are in her four-runner for this trip; the roads and area up north are incredibly muddy and unsafe. This thing has a center console, making it incredibly difficult to fluster her in other ways. I am super ready to get to the inn so I can take her clothes off and do beautiful things to her body.

There are many trails and walking paths up here, and I think I have found the best one for this trip, but I need to pretend I have no idea where we're going. When Mount Kineo comes into view, I look over to Kira knowingly. "Hmmm, Moosehead Lake, huh?" She whips her head my way in outrage.

"HOW DID YOU KNOW!" She yells, "Did Ollie tell you?! I am going to kill him!"

"Kira, I can see Mt Kineo from here!" I explain as I point to the mountain nestled on the far side of Moosehead Lake.

"Oh well, yes, we're going to Moosehead Lake." The eye-roll that came out of her when she said that was palpable. I can't help but laugh, which causes another way of pink to climb up her beautiful neck.

"Do I get to know where we are staying? Or is it a surprise?" I ask full well, knowing the answer to my question.

"Fine, we're staying at the Chamberlain Hill Inn…" she whispers. "It's super pretty and on the top end of the budget for this weekend, but I wanted to go all out." She takes a deep breath, "The last six months have been so stressful, with the Dodds, with work, with the fucking snow… I just wanted something luxurious for this weekend."

"Honey, that sounds wonderful, but why did you choose that inn?" I question, genuinely curious.

"I chose it because of the exterior. It is a big, beautiful white estate perched on a hill's side. Along the hillside, there is a beautiful retaining wall that is twenty feet tall and made of beautiful stone that extends nine hundred feet. The estate overlook is stunning, and there are private walking trails, a spa, and a gourmet restaurant… I just had to." She looks at me with so much love, "I love you, and I wanted this for us."

She is the most caring woman I have ever had the opportunity to love. She has helped me with so much and opened her heart to me after everything that has happened in her life… I feel so fortunate to be here with her.

"It sounds perfect, sugar plum; I can't wait to get there." I lean across the center console and kiss her cheek. We settle into silence and listen to the bizarre murder, and it is perfect.

Chapter Twenty-Three

One week ago…

Ben

I am about to do one of the scariest things I have ever done in my entire life. *It's okay, he likes you, everything will be alright.* I tell myself as I pull into the drive and walk up the front steps. I pull open the storm door and knock. Stepping back, I wait. It is about 5 p.m. I know they are home because the cars are in the driveway, but I am still unsure. I hear footsteps getting closer to the door; I've been holding my breath, I notice as the front door opens. "Ben, what a surprise. Is Kira okay?" Mr. Logan looks worried.

"Oh yes, Mr. Logan, Kira is great. She is working late tonight, but I wanted to know if I could talk to you and your wife?" I remarked. Mr. Logan's eyebrows shot up in surprise.

"Why, yes, of course, Ben, come on in." He turned and shouted, "NORA, BEN IS HERE." I took a deep, centering breath and went in, clutching my pocket, which contained a small velvet box like it was the key to saving my life. We walk into the living room and sit down. In my wildest dreams, I had never thought I would ever be here, never really thought marriage was something I genuinely wanted. With Kira, I need it all.

"Good evening; sorry for dropping in unannounced. I know it is almost dinner time, but I just wanted to see you before our weekend away, and this is the only night Kira is doing an evening shift." I say, nerves coating every word. I am relatively sure I am shaking right now.

"Oh, Ben, it's fine," Nora says. "Can I get you something to drink? Or are you hungry?" She asks, ever the host.

"Oh no, thank you, Mrs. Logan." I take a deep breath, "I came to see you; I know Kira has been married before, and I don't know if that prick asked for your permission."

Mr. Logan cuts me off, "He did, and I regret every day giving it to him." Anger lacing every word, he says, "What makes you bring that up, Ben?" His expression changes from wrath to one of… what is that? Knowing? *He knows what I am going to ask… Breathe.* I tell myself, or I am going to pass out right here.

"Well, I bought a ring," Mrs. Logan sucks in an audible breath at my announcement.

"Did you bring it!" Her voice is one of glee and happiness.

"Yes, I did." I take the deep blue velvet ring box out. Opening it slowly to show them, "It's a 1-carat oval diamond with three round smaller diamonds nestled on either side." I say, "I picked it out myself… My mom and I went, and I got to design it."

"It is stunning. I have seen Kira's dream boards, and it is almost identical to one I know she loves." Mrs. Logan, tears glistening in her eyes, looks over at Mr. Logan and back to me and the velvet box. "You have our blessing," They say in unison.

I let out the most prolonged breath of my entire life; tears are on the edges of my vision. "I promise I will give your daughter everything; I promise to make her happy and ensure she gets everything she has ever wanted in life." I express proudly, "I will never let her hurt or feel new pains if it's the last thing I do… I will care for her even when her past tries to climb back in." I admit, "I love her… I have since the first day I laid eyes on her."

"We know; we saw the change in her the first day she came home after you saved her on Main Street." Mrs. Logan says, "We're happy to see our daughter sparkle again."

Mr. Logan does not usually say much but says, "Ben, you are a diligent man who makes my daughter incredibly happy. I no longer believe in giving blessings, but I would give them to you if I did. I do not own my daughter; this is not the 18th century any longer. But, you are a wonderful decision. I hope she says yes." The tears in his eyes are on the edge of boiling over. Kira told me her father was the emotional one; I never expected this much emotion. If we have a daughter, I imagine I would feel the same, especially with all the hurt Kira has faced in the last decade…

With that, I get everything ready to go for the weekend. The first step was talking to Ollie to get all the details and loop him in on what was happening. Ollie and I do not have a fantastic relationship; we are vastly different people, but we love Kira. He sent over all the information he retrieved from Kira, unsuspecting and oblivious to what we were planning. I wished they had a willow tree on the inn's grounds. That would make this perfect.

***

Present day...

Kira

"Well, here we are," I say in absolute awe of this incredible structure. I look at Ben; he has not taken his eyes off the building and its expansive grounds.

"It's amazing. I can't believe how large that retaining wall is, and it looks beautifully restored from out here." He replies, a voice in awe of his surroundings.

"Let's get inside. I am beat and want to bathe in the massive soaking tubs!" I whisper-yell to Ben.

"Sounds good to me. Is there room for me there? Or do I get to watch?" He growls into my ear before he exits the car to grab our bags.

"Guess we'll have to see!" I jump out and make my way toward the expansive inn. "He was a Civil War General." I had never heard of him until I started researching inns and bed and breakfasts. I knew Ben is interested in history, and the property is gorgeous, so he would love it here as much as I knew I would. With that, we headed up the stairs onto the grand wraparound porch; a pump woman opened the door to welcome us.

"Good afternoon. My name is Pamela, but you can call me Pan!" "Welcome to the Chamberlain Hill Inn." Her singing voice was pleasant to listen to.

"Good afternoon, Pam!" I gush with joy. "We are so happy to be here; the property is gorgeous."

"Well, thank you! We love it here. Let me get you all checked in, and you can get settled or even go on an adventure!" Pam hustles to the counter and logs us into the computer. She hands us a beautiful key. It is bronze with an intricate flower decoration on the key's bow. It looks like a rose or a carnation. "You're in room 7; it has a wonderful view of the grounds, the mountains, and Moosehead Lake." She says, "We hope you enjoy your stay. There is staff here 24/7. If you need anything, call down." With that, we follow the signs. We are on the second floor. There are two rooms on the first, three on the second, and two on the third. I am pretty pleased to be on the second floor. I'm not too fond of stairs and would have been happy on the first floor, for that matter, but it is perfect.

We walk into our gorgeous room. There was a four-poster bed with fluffy white bedding, and it took all my effort not to climb into it and sleep! We walk hand in hand into the bathroom to see the clawfoot-deep soaking tub. There is indeed room for both Ben and me. Without a beat, we are both stripping naked and climbing into the tub. "We probably should have let it fill up before we got in here, ha-ha-ha." I cannot stop laughing as we sit in this cold tub, slowly waiting for the water to cover us with hot water.

Ben is sputtering with laughter and with a bit of chatter to his teeth from the cold. "It probably would have been better, but your body keeps me a little warm." He says into my ear; he begins to lick the spot below my ear that he knows drives me crazy. As he does, I start to feel a hardening of his length against my back, which is just another form of torture.

"Why are we in this tub anyway? Let us get out and show me what you do best with that tongue, Benjamin Barnett." I say with more sass than I expected.

"Yes, ma'am," He says, lifting me out of the tub. Forgoing the towel and tossing me onto the bed. He lands with a squeak, "You know we've never had sex in a bed like this before." The devilish grin that takes over his face is glorious. "I know a way to keep you from squirming out of my grip," His eyes fill with lust and a grin as wide as can be. "Do you remember our safe word?

"Pineapple" I say with an eyebrow raised and arms already behind my head in anticipation. Ben disappears into the bathroom; he finds a few extra pillowcases and a sheet in the linen closet. He went to work fastening the fabric to my wrists, not too hard but enough that I would not slip out. Once he finished, I watch as he kisses his way down my entire body. The restraints make it torturous; I want to touch him, run my hands through his hair, and force him down… Down to my throbbing clit.

"Are you ready for me, baby?" He growled, not to me but to my entrance. With a long lick, we both moan savagely. *I hope these walls are soundproof; I made no promises to be quiet.* I think to myself, between moans, licks, and sucking, *I might combust right here. We are in the most romantic room of my entire life, and the man of my dreams is devouring me.* Ben works his fingers inside me while he licks and bites pulling the orgasm out of me. I was on the edge, teetering in and out of sanity, when he whispered into my pussy again, "Cum for me, baby."

That was all I needed, "BEN! FUCK!," I whisper-screamed as I could not cover my face and mouth. This was not the place for a loud, earth-shattering orgasm, but fuck it. *I love this man and will scream his name no matter how fancy the place we are staying at is.* I can hear myself thinking as I slowly come back down to reality. He finally sits back on his feet; reaching down, he undoes my feet. Leaving my hands tied, he brings my legs up onto each shoulder; I think, my feet behind his head, and I wait.

"I'm just going to take care of you tonight, Kira." The way he says my name takes my breath away, as he nudges his cock against my swollen clit, I might cum again just from the contact alone.

"Yes, please, baby," I am panting. He drags his cock over my clit, drenched by my wetness. Back and forth, back and forth he drags it... I am beginning to see stars again when he pulls back and slams into me. Taking my breath away, he holds my ass and makes me his repeatedly. Fucking me so thoroughly that I melt, completely sated, and sexed so well that I could go to sleep right now.

"I'm close," He says, "can I come all over your sexy tits baby?" He asks me, eyes hooded, cheeks flushed, and hands white, knuckling my hips.

"Yes, Ben, cover me in your cum." I rasp out.

"I'm...I'm cuu-ming," He moans out and drops my legs around his waist. Holding himself up with one hand and holding his cock in the other, he cums all over my chest as his orgasm pulses through him over and over. Once he finishes, he climbs out of the bed and pads into the bathroom once again. He retrieves a washcloth and starts the tub again. He returna to the bedroom and began to wipe me clean, untying my hands. Finally, we are both relaxing in the claw foot soaker tub; I am genuinely beyond happy and content with this life I am living now.

Chapter Twenty-Four

Ben

I wake up before Kira this morning and sneak into the inn's lobby. I find a younger-looking man sitting at the desk. He must be the night guy. "Good morning, sir. I'm staying in room 7, and I have a few questions,"

"Of course, how can I help you?" He responds. With that, I tell him my plan, and he begins to get everything ready, with the help of a couple hundred-dollar bills for his trouble.

***

Kira

I wake up, and Ben was not there; he probably went to get us coffee. I roll over and fall back into a quiet sleep. I have not had any nightmares in a long time, no longer fearing for my life in my dreams. No more self-doubt. I love this man, and we needed this weekend—just us.

I hear the key of the door and open my eyes. Looking over, I see the handsome man I love. "Good morning, honey," He whispers with coffee in each hand. "How'd you sleep?"

"Hmmm, that coffee smells wonderful. I slept like a baby, how about you?" I ask, reaching for him and the coffee. He bends down and kisses my forehead, handing me the warm, delicious-smelling coffee.

"Well, I am excited to explore with you this weekend. It is going to be so nice out today and tomorrow, " he says with such enthusiasm. It was nice to see him out of work mode. I told him this was a stress-free weekend, and he was doing just that: relaxing. Relaxed and sexy Ben is my favorite Ben.

"Do you want to go have breakfast downstairs in the dining room and then go for a drive or walk?" I ask, curious about what we're going to get into this weekend. I planned this visit, but I did not want there to be an itinerary to cause stress.

"Food sounds great, and maybe we can save the walk for this evening? Why don't we go down to the beach when it's cooler? Maybe swim a bit today?" He says, smiling at me, causing the most enormous butterflies to flutter around my tummy.

"Yes, please! I am not swimming in glacier-cold water, though. I will get dressed and pack our bag for the day." I say, and with that, we head on our way to breakfast and down to the beach.

"If you say so, it's like nature's Ice Bucket Challenge." He says with a shrug and a wink.

★★★

Ben

After breakfast, Kira let me drive her baby into town, and we followed the signs to Lily Bay State Park. There is an extensive warm brown sandy area that runs along the lake.

There is so much nature here; deer are just grazing, and I can see otters playing as we make our way to the park. Once we park, we find the shade of a tree and get settled in. I am not a beach person; I'm not too fond of the sand, but I know that Kira loves it. She is a reader; she only goes somewhere with book options. She gets all cozy on the beach blanket, looking beautiful in a wine color bikini top and floral bottom with a similar wine color weaved throughout. Her porcelain skin will burn a bit, but the rosiness of her cheeks is so endearing.

"Are you going to read for a while, baby?" I ask; she looks up and nods. Once she gets sucked into a book, getting words out of her is hard unless I pull her entirely out and take the book away ha-ha. I laugh and walk away, "I'm going to look around and see what I can find by the water," I say over my shoulder to her. She nods some more, and I do just that. She loves shells and rocks; I do my best, but this beach is clean. There is not so much as a cigarette to be found in the sand.

After walking for a long while, I decide to walk back. My stomach growls, and I know Kira has packed snacks. I make my way over to her; she comes into sight, and she is beautiful. Her lovely hair is all to one side, her arm resting over her chin, and her glasses on the bridge of her nose. She hasn't seen me yet. During this walk, I thought about many things: my plan for tonight and this girl right here.

***

Later that day...

Kira

We are going out to dinner; he told me he had planned to have dinner with the inn and brought a picnic somewhere as a surprise. I have on a fresh sundress. Since it is spring and there was a slight chill in the air, I wear a warm wrap. He wears his usual black jeans, warm flannel, and a grey undershirt. He grabs a blanket just in case I get cold. "Are you ready to go, Sugar Plum?" Ben asks, love in his eyes.

"Oh yes, I am starving. Where are we going to be eating our "picnic"? I ask curiously.

He smiles that handsome smile I love so much. "It's a surprise, but we do need to walk there. It isn't far, but you'll see," He admits with a twinkle in his eyes.

"Lead the way, handsome," I take his hand. We make our way down the hill of the massive estate and see the beautiful retaining wall wrapping along the ridge below the inn. We follow a well-worn trail made wide enough for a four-wheeler or side-by-side. Solar lights line the trail, and it is so picturesque. A breeze is in the air; Ben wraps his warm arm around me as we walk. Listening to the birds settle in for the evening, the tiny critters making their way home in the trees. There is rustling in the leaves. Low music gets a little louder the further we get down the trail. It is not any one song in particular, but the songs are all of my favorite. I look up at Ben, and he smiles. "What do you have planned, Mr. Barnett?" I ask, a little uneasy. My stomach flips a bit, and my hand becomes clammy in his.

"You'll see." That was all he says as we walk through a large steel arbor. It is stunning. With intricate steel vines running up and over, I did not even notice what was beyond the arbor until Ben stops walking. "What do you think?" He asks, his voice sounding unsure. Nervous?

"Oh my," I see a small cast iron table with a tablecloth. On the table is a meal fit for royalty; there are even little shining cloches over the largest of each plate. "It is amazing! How did you plan this?" I ask, turning… Then I see it: we are in a grove of cherry trees. They bloomed recently, and their flowers were spectacular in the low light; there were small solar lights on the ground illuminating them. We walk a bit further into the grove of trees, where there is a bench. Ben walks to me and has me sit down; I was in awe. I have never been around this many blossoming trees, let alone cherry trees. It is as if we were transported to Japan or D.C. with all the stunning blooms. I sit down, waiting for Ben to join me, but he does not. I look up, confused, and there is his.

Down on one knee before me, holding a deep blue velvet box. I am awe-struck again. There are not even words to explain my surprise. "Kira Logan, you are the sunshine on all my rainy days, the joy to my life, and the person who makes me so incredibly happy. I know we have not been together that long, but I love you; I have loved you since that day when you almost got run over on Main St." He explains with tears in the corners of his eyes and his hands shaking. "I had never expected to find such a kind, generous, and hard-working woman like you in a million years, Kira. You make me want to be the best man I can be for you; you make every day an adventure, and if I am honest, our sex is the best." That made me chuckle, with tears streaming down both of our cheeks. "I have never felt this way about anyone, and I never want to feel this way about anyone else." His voice cracked, "Kira, will you make me the happiest man alive and marry me?" Not giving him a chance to think, I would say no, I jump off the bench!

"OH MY GOD! YES! BEN YES!" Squealing, he opens the velvet box, and I cannot breathe. He bought the ring of my dreams, an oval cut with diamonds nestled on either side in a white gold band. It is perfect. "Oh, Ben, it's beautiful," I tell him, "It is perfect." I am full-on ugly, crying now, kissing him, tears everywhere, running down my face as he attempts to place the ring on my shaking hand.

"Kira, you need to stop crying so I can put this ring on!" He said it with only a little bit of sarcasm. "Are you still hungry?" He asks, knowing I am shaking because he had made my heart grow infinitely larger but also because I was starving.

"Of course, what's for dinner?" My stomach protests at how long it's taking me to get food into my belly. We sit at the table, and I open my sterling silver cloche. Inside is a ham and provolone Italian sub with little slices of green peppers and salt and vinegar chips. "You know me too well, Benjamin Barnett."

"I do, future Kira Barnett." He kisses me soundly, and we eat together in the cherry grove with the sun completely cresting the horizon, leaving us in the light of the solar lights twinkling around us.

Chapter Twenty-Five

Kira

I call Penny in the car as we are on our way back from Moosehead. "Oh my god, no way!" She squeals. "Have you guys picked a date yet?"

"No, not yet! I just wanted to ask you something. I know it's super soon to ask. It isn't the most adorable way to ask, but will you be my Matron of Honor?" I ask tentatively.

"Kira, Absolutely, yes! I will be your Matron of Honor!" Penny says in her sweet, kind voice. "I cannot wait! Do you have anyone else you want to have at the wedding party? Or are you just doing Best Man and Matron of Honor?" She asks. I look over to Ben; he gives me this look that could only say whatever you want, babe.

"Well, I do want one other person to be in it. Her name is Paysen Scott. She is my first cousin and lives in Kent, England." I say, "We will have to give her enough notice so it doesn't cost an arm and a leg to get her over here for the wedding."

"Oh, that is wonderful! I cannot wait to meet her." Penny says, always so enthusiastic, "When will you ask her to be at the wedding party?"

"When I find someone to be next to Ben's brother Conrad," I reply flatly. Ben has few friends so it will be a short list.

"What about Marshall?" Penny asks, "He did help win the case, and y'all spent a lot of time together prepping." She is correct, but will Ben be okay with that? That's the real question we need to be asking.

"Penny, I am so excited for you to be my Matron of Honor! I will ask Ben what he thinks about that," I say, looking over at the man in question. He raises an eyebrow in response, waiting for more information. "I will let you know if we decide on a date and size! I love you! See you at game night this weekend." I am so happy she said yes...

"What will Ben need to decide on?" He asks in the third person like a psychopath.

"Oh, if you're okay with Marshall being a groomsman to make the number even." I rush out quickly, with a crinkle of my eyelids, waiting for his response. His eyebrows furrowed in a small response, looking at me, then back at the highway before him.

"Well, Conrad is my Best Man? Why do I need anyone else?" He asks.

"Well, I was hoping Paysen would be able to fly over and be my bridesmaid alongside Penny," I say quietly, making my voice tiny for sympathy. "It would look weird with two on the right and three on the left." Symmetry is essential to a custom home builder, and I hope that will sway him. For good measure, I push my bottom lip out and make big eyes at him, "Pwwease."

"For you, yes." He says, looking at me now without looking back, "Because I love you, and that lip looks very kissable." I feel the heat rush down my body between my thighs. When he looks at me with those lust-filled eyes and gives me what I want... He knows exactly how to get what he wants, too.

The next day, I started looking at dates and times in October and coordinating with Paysen. When I ask her to be a bridesmaid, her exact words were, "I get to plan the hen do, and we are going to get smashed." Her British is showing all over the place. I cannot wait for her to meet Marshall. I have yet to tell her about him because it's Marsh. Marsh is hot, serious, and a successful lawyer. Paysen is beautiful, intelligent, funny, and a big company magazine editor. He is originally from the state that dumped all 340 chests of tea into the Atlantic, and Paysen drinks tea. She is from the UK!

My phone rings, it is Paysen. "Hun, I have a conference in America in October. Do you think you could plan to have your wedding around then? I'm going to sound super selfish, but I don't want to have to make the trip twice. I will need to be at my conference on the 11th of October. Is that too soon?" She says with her elegant British accent.

"I was just going to ask what you thought of October!" I say with a bit too much squeal in my voice! "Would you want to do it before or after your conference?"

"Oh yes! I would definitely like to see you and be in your wedding before the conference." She says, "I want to have time to plan the hen do, so maybe I'll visit a week before your wedding?"

"Yes!" I squeal. "I'll talk to Ben tonight." I'm so excited to see her.

"Okay, great. I'll get it planned, and then you can let me know the definite date. Speak to you soon!" Paysen breezes as we get off the phone.

***

Two weeks later...

Ben

Kira is consumed with wedding planning; I have given my opinion on some things, but this is all for her. She gets what she wants; I want it to be smaller, and I want her to be happy. We have been living together, and it has been the best thing. I get come home to her every night and wake up next to her every morning. We have our routine now, and the growing pains have become more manageable. I need to meet with

Marsh today to discuss being my groomsman. He doesn't know about Paysen yet, and I don't plan on telling him.

Walking into Marshall's office in town, his older female secretary, Trudy, looks over her glasses at me. "Benjamin, nice to see you. I don't think you have an appointment today." She whispers as if that's as loud as her voice gets. "Do you need me, or are you here for Mr. Damien?"

"Here to see Marsh, is he busy?" I ask.

"He's not; you can head right up. I'll let him know you're coming." She tells me while preparing the intercom to let him know I am here. The office is located in an older building. I am almost positive it has been here since Main St. became a street. There are portions of brick and plaster that I can see, Marsh has made it very masculine here. There are dark wood tones, greys, and grey blues for accenting color, which can only be original hardwood floors with handmade nails. As I walk up the narrow staircase, the stairs creak slightly with my weight. At the top of the stairs are three doors; one is ajar: the bathroom, I note by the small white and black tiles peeking from the doorway. One of the three doors is closed, and the last is wide open, with a large dark wood desk.

"Ben! Nice to see you; what can I do for you today?" Marsh says with a touch of a Boston accent. It is only slightly present in his language now because he has been here so long.

"Not a lot. I have a question for you," I say hesitantly.

Marsh raises an eyebrow. "Really?" He asks curiously. I continue my path into the room in one of the genuinely nice black leather armchairs. Sitting down, I sink into luxury. It is the best *leather chair I have ever sat in,* I admit to myself.

"So, you know that Kira and I are getting married in the fall?" I respond. He nods in response, "Well, we are trying to make the numbers even on either side." I hesitate, "I need one more groomsman." I wait patiently as his eyebrows raise in surprise.

"Oh really, and you'd like me to fill that role?" He remarked.

"Yes," I say. *I don't particularly like the idea, but we need the numbers.* I chastise myself while attempting a placating smile.

"For Kira, I will." He looks me in the eyes, and that response catches my attention.

"Why, for Kira?" I try not to sound hostile, holding his stare and clenching my fist.

"Because you and I know full well, it is a request from her, not you; she worked hard on your case. I think I owe her for all that work." He says calmly. Moving his hand around in the air, gesturing that explains just that. He isn't wrong; Kira worked day and night to find alternatives to going to court and a healthy threat to get them back down and pay. Her gut feeling gave us the idea about the possible fraud, the idea that the Dodd's had no intention of ever fully paying me for the job's completion.

"You're right; I could care less." I shrug, "Whatever makes her happy."

"Who is her second? Penny is her MOH, but who is the other bridesmaid?" He inquired.

"Oh," *Do I tell him the truth?* "Her cousin, Paysen. She is not from around here." I say, hoping for no follow-up questions.

"Interesting, well I look forward to the wedding." He winks, sits back, and crosses his arms. "Have you picked a date yet?"

"She is working on it. Paysen has a tight schedule, and she's a must for Kira whenever she is available." I explain, "We should have a date soon." With that, I stand and make my way towards the exit. I stop in the doorway and turn, "Thank you, Marsh, for everything."

"You're welcome, Ben, it's a pleasure." He says without any pity on his face, "Send Trudy the details; if you don't, it won't end up on my calendar, and I will most likely forget." With that, he gets back to his paperwork, and I leave the building.

Chapter Twenty-Six

Kira

Ben arrives home at the usual time, and I greet him outside as I do daily while the dogs do their business. He climbs out of his truck, eyes never leaving mine as he approaches me. He always looks at me like I am going to be the last thing he sees before he dies, wanting to take in every part of me. "Hey, handsome," I purr into his ear as he hugs me.

"Hey, beautiful, do you want to go for a walk to the willow?" He asks, love in his eyes.

"Yes, it is hot, and the dogs could use a swim," I respond; I *am hot too, but for other reasons.* With that response, he takes my hand, and I whistle for the dogs. We stroll down the path to the first place he ever took me when we met. "Did you get to talk to Marsh today?" I ask.

"Yes, he's in, but not for me." He claims, "Your hard work made quite an impression on him."

"Oh really, the famous Marshall Damien was happy to have my help?" I inquire.

"Apparently so," He shrugs with a sly smile on his luscious lips. "He asked about Paysen. Will you warn her about him and his charms, or will you let them meet organically?"

"I will just let it happen. If I am correct, they will hit it off and fall madly in love." I smile ear to ear. "That way, she will be forced to move to America and be close to me." I am selfish; I should not play matchmaker, but they are perfect for each other. Both are incredibly hardworking, beautiful people, *and I loved one of them!* I think while smiling.

"We will have to see; what if they hate each other?" He does have a point, but I will not let that deter me. "They won't. She loves me, and he appreciates me, and we will arrange their meeting in a way that will make it seem like we had no idea they are perfect for each other." I shrug, "It has to be their idea, or it won't happen."

"Using psychology against them, are you going to plant the idea? Or talk each of them up to each other separately?" He asks, concerned. *He knows what I am going to say.*

"Well…" I say with a shy smile and make my eyes doe-like and big. "I was hoping you'd talk up Marsh to Paysen, and I'd talk up Paysen to Mash." He runs a hand through his hair in apparent tension.

"Babe, you know I'm uncomfortable with that kind of stuff… I don't know Paysen; how will I talk to her?" He places both hands in his pocket; he does this when he is stressed, and it keeps him from fidgeting with his hands.

"That is it! She is just like me! You will love her… But not too much, or I will cut you." I joke, "Should we have her visit early? It is the middle of August already we only have a few months to plan if we decide on October."

"I would say just let her come when she says, and we'll take it from there. Marsh needs a date so Trudy can put it in his schedule." He reminds me, I found a date!

"I have a date! October 8th is perfect. It is a Sunday; we can spend the week on the beach or by the pool." I gave him a knowing look; he hates sand.

"Works for me, I'll call Trudy tomorrow." With that, he takes my face in his hands; I notice we have made it to the spot where he took me and made me his. He kisses me deeply and thoroughly, and I melt into him. Feeling every inch of his hot body against mine, I feel his hands moving down my body when he pulls me up into a bride carry and starts moving towards the pond.

"NO, NO, NO, BEN!" I scream *he is going to throw me in the fucking pond.*

"Shhh… you're hot. I am just going to cool you off." He purrs in my ear, holding me tightly so I cannot fight against him. *If I am going in, so is he!* Once we are close enough to the water, he gets ready to toss me and let go, but before he can fully let go, I grab hold like a spider monkey and drag him in with me and in we go. "SHIT!"

We splash into the water and come sputtering up for air. I gaze into his eyes and say, "I love you." He pulls me in tighter.

"I love you, Kira; I can't wait to be your husband." He says honestly. His expression says it all; soft, loving eyes look back at me. *I am genuinely the luckiest girl in the world.*

Epilogue

October 7th ...

Paysen & Marshall

I can't believe I have to pretend not to hate that idiot I will have to walk down the aisle with. Marshall Damien, I haven't had the heart to tell Kira that he and I will never be together. Not after what happened five years ago. He dares to act like he has no fucking idea who I am. So, here I am at the pub down the way from the venue, in Northern Maine, of all places. I am drinking red wine; it is my safest alcohol. I drink it slower than any other alcohol. Kira would never forgive me if I showed up to her wedding hungover.

I hear the bell jingle over the door to the pub and turn to look at the newcomer. It's half past 8, and I should be leaving soon. My breath catches because, really… In walks the pain in my ass himself. Marshall Damien makes eye contact with me and heads to the bar where I sit. "Paysen," he inclines his head, "Seat taken?" *Obviously, it's not, but whatever. Be polite, Paysen; you have 24 hours left here.* I chastise myself because I have many things to say to this man.

"Marshall. No, it isn't taken." I reply, moving my handbag from the stool to the other stool on the opposite side of me. I look forward, counting the bottles on the back wall. *1, 2, 3, 4, 5… breath Paysen.*

"How's it going? Are you ready for tomorrow?" He asks after he orders his beer and turns on his stool beside me. *Breathe.*

"Yep, I'm ready to get to work next week and then fly home." I reply, "I'm so glad Kira is happy, but I'm ready to head home." The shock on Marshall's face is evident.

"You're leaving?" He asks, "When?" I turn my head to look, and he seems a bit put out that I am leaving.

"I'm leaving either tomorrow night or early Monday morning. Why?" I ask, truly curious why he would even care.

"Oh." Was all he said to me, concern in his eyes. "I thought… maybe." I cut him off right there.

"Don't." I interrupt, "You have barely said a word to me all week. Not when I arrived and not at any of the dinners and rehearsals we have been to." I take a calming breath and stand, leaving my cash on the bar. "If you wanted to talk to me, you had the opportunity, and lastly, I don't want anything to do with you." I sound like just another crazy British woman out of breath when I make my way out into the cool fall air. It is almost dark, but I can see the inn up on the hill. I hear the crunching of gravel behind me... *Don't look back, don't stop... Keep walking.*

★★★

Marshall

She just got up and left... It didn't register in my brain that she was going until I heard the bells over the door. I throw some cash down and leave my full beer sitting there on the counter. I can see her; she's making her way back up to the inn in her patterned wrap dress that enhances all of her beautiful curves. It almost makes me stop my chase to reach her; she has been driving me crazy this entire time she has been in Maine. *How on earth is Paysen Scott, the woman I spent three magical days in North Carolina five years ago?*

Looking back, it was all I had been doing for that past week; I couldn't let on that I knew her. I couldn't let my friends see that I was a mess. I am a lawyer; I have an image to uphold in this town, hell, this county. I cannot let women take entirely over my thoughts, but that's what happened.

"Poppy, come back to bed," I tell her as she stands in the window of the hotel room we have barely left. Only to eat and go to our conference. She is the most beautiful, alluring woman I have ever seen. She looks back over her shoulder at me, her brown waves cascading down her back.

"I will, Marsh, just taking in the view one more time before we head off to sleep," she says with her lovely British accent, which makes my stomach flip whenever she talks. I feel like a teenager who has figured out that women are more than just our friends. She makes her way over to me, her hazel eyes shining in the low sunset light. The light left shining around her head makes her look like a goddess.

"Perfect now, come here, let me touch you," I say, holding her wrist.

I snap back to reality; I made it to her. I had her wrist in my hand. "Marshall Damien, you will let me go this instant." She growls in that luscious accent. I can't help but smile; I didn't let go.

"Paysen, please. Wait. You need to hear me out." I beg, but she cuts me off.

"I have to do no such thing," She yanks her arm away from me and takes a few steps back. "You left. No word, no number, nothing! You made me feel like a fool." She has tears in the corners of her eyes, which she blinks away before they can even think about falling.

"I did, I know; I am so sorry." I explain, "I went back... I looked for you." *I looked everywhere, from the hotel to the conference hall, and even bought a bogus ticket to make it through security to catch her. It would have been a story to tell our grandchildren about.*

"No, you didn't, don't lie. You, Mr. Damien, got what you wanted from me and left. I am beyond it; it was five years ago, but if you think I will let you into my life. You are sorely mistaken." With that, she turned and headed up the hill. I ruined any chance I ever had with Paysen Scott. She was who

I had dreamt about for the last five years, regretting every decision I had ever made.

***

Paysen

The wedding went off without a hitch! Kira and Ben looked incredibly happy; they laughed, cried, and danced. Ben stopped being stubborn and danced with Kira in front of everyone, holding her and looking at her like she was the reason he breathed. There was one time in my life when I thought I could have that, but I have realized lately... I do not need it. I have my job, my friends, and my family.

I had to not only walk down the aisle with Marshall Damien, but I also had to sit next to him the entire meal. I don't think I have ever been more uncomfortable in my life. I hope it doesn't show in the pictures, for Kira's sake, but he kept looking at me. Looking at me with no expression, when I would look over at him and catch him, he would blush; there would be something in his eyes. I saw. Was it regret or guilt? I wasn't sure about those chestnut brown eyes, which twinkled with flecks of gold around the iris.

I did not let myself drink too much at the late lunch reception; I wanted to be out of Maine as fast as possible. I took the only cab available in the tiny town and headed for Bangor, Maine. The closest airport, I don't know if they would have a flight I could hop on, but it was worth a shot. I wasn't headed anywhere tiny. I was headed to Colorado Springs, Colorado. I'd be okay if I could at least get a flight heading in that direction. I needed to be in Colorado by the 10th of October, which gave me 48 hours to do so. I could drive, but the roads in America are fucking huge; I would absolutely die if I tried.

I love flying, especially when the only seat left on the plane is in first class. I had to pay for it, but I have points from frequent flying to pay for most of the cost. On the plane ride, I was able to read and relax. They had sparkling wine and crisps; no one knew who I was or where I was going. It was perfect, just me and "A Court of Silver Flames," Kira was kind enough to lend me her copy of the book since I forgot mine back in the UK. I will write to my boss when I arrive to say I'll be extending my stay in Colorado for a week after the conference. I need a vacation, and the mountains of Colorado sound wonderful.!

For, Paysen and Marshall's story keep an eye out for the second book, in the Hamlin County Series

About The
Author

Kate Blake

Hello, everyone thank you so much for taking the time to read this novel. My name is Kate Blake, I am a state of Maine native and wouldn't change it for the world. I am not a full-time writer, but maybe one day. I'm a mother, a wife, an ultrasound tech, a concrete business partner, an Air Force veteran, and finally, a published author. I have always wanted to be an author, and here I am, finally publishing a novel that, in a form, has lived in my mind for many years. The next book in the series is something I have never done: complete fiction; this story has aspects of my 30 years of life and a lot of dramatized fiction added in. "Finding Poppy" follows the journey of Paysen Scott and Marshall Damien on their second chance romance; there are issues from their past that they both need to get through. A feisty Brit and a New England charmer, how will their story play out? You'd have to take a peak at the bonus chapter from "Finding Poppy."

This story told the tale of a girl who has been close to my heart for many years. She lived through very similar experiences to Kira Logan; like Kira, she found love and is living happily ever after. I wanted to take the time to tell you all that you matter; no one should ever treat you like you do not. It is going to be hard, but you can save yourself; if you can't, there are resources for you. You can text BEGIN to 88788 or call the National Domestic Violence Hotline at 800-799-7233. You are never alone; I know it may feel that way, but you aren't. If you ever feel unsafe or need help, do not hesitate to contact NDVH.

On a lighter note, this story has remained unfinished in my mind until recently, and I am so excited to share this series with the world. I am very excited to see what Paysen Scott and Marshall Damien have in store. If you loved this book as much as I loved writing it, leave a review or post. Don't forget to tag me @moodreadingwithkate.

"Finding Poppy"

October 9th...

Paysen

After one connection in LaGuardia, New York, I finally landed in Denver, Colorado, after seven and a half hours of traveling. I am so ready to be in my hotel room. I am wrecked and prepared for a cuppa of tea and a steaming hot shower. I paid extra for the first class from LaGuardia because they don't have that on the smaller aircraft. The six hours in first class involved multiple glasses of champagne and the best biscuits I've had in quite a long while. I checked my phone when we landed. I have a few missed messages from Kira, who is Kira Barnett now. My beautiful cousin got married yesterday, and I took off before she went off on her honeymoon. I could not stay any longer. I cringe when opening my phone.

> Kira 09:00 [Pays, where are you? I got up to leave, and you weren't here.]

> Kira 09:05 [I have looked everywhere for you, and the inn said you checked out]

> Kira 09:06 [Are you safe?]

> Kira 10:00 [I checked your location, and it says you're in New York...]

> Kira 16:12 [Now you're in Colorado... You're either on your way to your conference or have been kidnapped by a serial killer who forgot to shut off your shared location with me. I am not impressed with his murdering skills. I hope you're safe, call me when you're free. I am on my way to Aruba, so if I don't respond immediately, I probably didn't get kidnapped and murdered like you. xxx]

That made me chuckle, this girl. *I have only known of her existence briefly, and she has already weaseled her way into my heart. She is sunshine and love, and I, on the other hand, am practical and do my best to keep my emotions in check.*

Paysen 17:00 [I am alive, did not get taken. I made it to Colorado! Sorry, I left so unexpectedly. It's a long story that I'll tell you after your honeymoon, Mrs. Barnett! Enjoy xx!]

Hopefully, that will stay her worry. I took a cab to my luxury stay at the most excellent place in downtown Denver. I have a couple extra days before the conference and cannot wait. I will be forgetting all about Marshall Damien all over again. Why he couldn't ignore me the entire time is beyond me. I will not allow him back into my heart again, for him to inevitably break it. I tell myself I will enjoy these few days. Enjoy this conference and stay for an extra week. I will enjoy everything Colorado has to offer me.

That night, I plan my itinerary with a glass of red wine and the rest of "A Court of Silver Flames." I also need to update my blog... I have taken a week off from writing to my adoring fans: adoring, ha-ha, the very few who read my blog religiously. Still, I should give an update tomorrow afternoon, maybe. I tell myself that even with my full-time job, writing on my blog, "Poppy Speaks," is something that truly brings me joy.

Tomorrow, I'll write; tomorrow, I chastise. Back to my agenda: the spa day. In the morning, there will be a facial and mani-pedi, a relaxing massage, and a sweat in the sauna. I will feel perfectly refreshed for my first day at the conference. It is a week-long of briefings, slide shows, and people trying to sell their latest everything. There will most likely be editing equipment and new publishers, and a legal team will come in to speak on copyright, plagiarism, and contracts.

If I could go through the entire conference without looking at or speaking to another lawyer, I would. For some reason, I have a bad taste in my mouth for lawyers and their lawyerly ways. I replay that night with Marshall a lot. There are times in my memory when he comes back to me and makes everything right. Then reality set in, and I knew that it was just a fantasy—a fantasy that could never happen. We live on the other side of the ocean from each other.

I finish my lists, get everything ready for the next couple of days, and fall into a deep sleep; thank you to my trusty red wine they had at the hotel bar. *I open my eyes; I am not where I am when I lay my head on the overstuffed hotel pillow. There is a hard, warm chest beneath my ear. I can hear the slow rhythmic thumping of a heart, thump, thump, thump, thump. I sit up slowly; it can't be. I can't be here; I look around the ocean-themed hotel room. I smell the ocean from the open sliding glass door as the dim haze of dawn shines through the windows. "Marshall," I whisper. He doesn't so much as stir. I look around; I am thrown back five years to the lovely three days that we spent together. I have had this dream before; this is the day before he leaves and never returns. Leaves while I am asleep and blissful. He leaves and doesn't so much as leave a note. That was why I gave him a fake name, right? This was only a one-time thing, which I told myself as I gave him my name. I knew who he was because he was a speaker at the conference: Marshall Damien, an East Coast contract lawyer from Maine. I had seen his name on the pamphlet when we received the itinerary, but I never expected I'd end up here. I am just resting my head on his beautiful chest.*

With a gust of breath, I shoot straight up in my bed; I am awake now. I am alone in my hotel room in Denver, Colorado. I guess I am not over this issue of Marshall Damien, but I need to be; this is supposed to be a getaway for me… It was not a blast from the past to drag me back down to that time five years ago. Maybe I'll take my friend Sandra's advice and get underneath someone else to get over him. It has been a long while, but I have tried her advice before.

Acknowledgements

Thank you to my husband Brandon for having the confidence in me to achieve any dream I set my mind to. Thank you to my Mom and Dad for giving me the drive to achieve those goals. I have watched them crush all their goals in life, and I have tried to do the same. My father also published his first novel this year, "Ageless" by Jon Lewis, and I couldn't be prouder. His ability to achieve that goal gave me the final push to get this done to my siblings, who always have the confidence in me to get things done, specifically my younger brother Owen. He makes me proud by working hard and using his creativity in the theater world. I may not be a theater gal, but I am so proud of him and all of the hard work he has put into his craft. To my Mother-in-law, who isn't a huge reader but will literally read anything I write because she loves me enough, too. She has been in my corner, waiting patiently for that paperback copy. To my best friend Niki, thank you for being there, helping with all the storylines, and always being my hype girl. You always make me feel fabulous, even when I think it sounds terrible or too much! To my cousin Paige, our relationship is a new one. We didn't even know each other existed for decades, but we can't choose our family and how we got them. What we can choose is if we want them in our lives. She is across the ocean from me and has been here the whole time. She's read my notes and chapters, given my opinions, and helped me with all the British phrases and slang. I didn't choose her as my family, but I did choose her as my friend. I wouldn't change that for the world. Lastly, a community of people on IG, my Bookstagram besties, have been rooting for me from the start. They have offered to beta read for me, hype me up, and do all they can to get my novel seen. Thank you to all of these people and more I love so dearly.

Love, Kate

295